100 DRESSES

Ghost of a Chance

Also by Susan Maupin Schmid

If the Magic Fits (100 Dresses #1)

The Starlight Slippers (100 Dresses #3)

Lost Time

Ghost of a Chance

②

Susan Maupin Schmid

Illustrations by Lissy Marlin

A Yearling Book

Text copyright © 2017 by Susan Maupin Schmid
Cover art copyright © 2017 by Melissa Manwill
Interior illustrations copyright © 2017 by Lissy Marlin

All rights reserved. Published in the United States by Yearling, an imprint of
Random House Children's Books, a division of Penguin Random House LLC,
New York. Originally published in hardcover in the United States by
Random House Children's Books, New York, in 2017.

Yearling and the jumping horse design are registered
trademarks of Penguin Random House LLC.

Visit us on the Web! rhcbooks.com

Educators and librarians, for a variety of teaching tools,
visit us at RHTeachersLibrarians.com

The Library of Congress has cataloged the hardcover
edition of this work as follows:
Names: Schmid, Susan Maupin, author. | Marlin, Lissy, illustrator.
Title: Ghost of a chance / by Susan Maupin Schmid ; illustrated by
Lissy Marlin.
Description: New York : Random House Children's Books, [2017] |
Series: One hundred dresses ; book 2 | Summary: Darling Dimple,
a young orphan, must use the enchanted dresses to find the ghost
that is haunting the castle she calls home.
Identifiers: LCCN 2016011924 | ISBN 978-0-553-53373-6 (hardcover) |
ISBN 978-0-553-53374-3 (hardcover library binding) |
ISBN 978-0-553-53375-0 (ebook)
Subjects: | CYAC: Fairy tales. | Magic—Fiction. | Clothing and dress—
Fiction. | Ghosts—Fiction. | Castles—Fiction. | Orphans—Fiction. |
Humorous stories.
Classification: LCC PZ8.S2835 Gh 2017 | DDC [Fic]—dc23

ISBN 978-0-553-53376-7 (pbk.)

Printed in the United States of America
10 9 8 7 6 5 4 3 2 1
First Yearling Edition 2018

For my daughter Rebecca,
artist and shark aficionado

1

I slipped into Queen Candace's closet, gripping the canary's cage in my fist. My friend Roger hovered outside the door. Moonbeams silvered the dresses and poured across the rose-patterned carpet, bleaching it to blues and grays. The stained-glass canary in the great peaked-arch window shone like a lamplit jewel.

It had been three months since I'd exposed that thief—and imposter—Dudley. Three months of jumping and fetching, of pressing mountains of handkerchiefs, towels, and sheets, of doing a portion of the Wardrobe Mistress's job. But now things had settled down. The Princess had appointed a new Wardrobe Mistress, and I had a little free time.

A little free time and a closet full of unworn dresses.

Not to mention the promise I'd made Roger to show him my secret.

"Are you sure this is safe?" Roger asked.

"I'm sure," I said, motioning him inside the closet.

I set the birdcage on the small table by the window. Lyric chirped drowsily in a puddle of moonlight. A quiver ran through the waking dresses. One hundred of them hung on silver hangers marked with numbered gold badges. They had all belonged to Queen Candace, the grandmother of Princess Mariposa. And although the dresses had been in this closet for years, they looked as bright and as new as they had on the day they were put there. Well, all except for one, Eighteen; faded rags were all that remained of the original dress.

Roger sidled into the closet and eased the door shut.

"The others are all downstairs," I pointed out.

"Okay." Roger swept his cap off and ran his fingers through his sandy hair.

The dresses rattled their hangers. Roger jumped.

"Be nice," I told them. "You have a guest."

The dresses clattered their hangers more urgently. They'd helped me thwart Dudley and his accomplice, Cherice. Those two had meant to unleash the dragons chained to the castle roof. Instead, Dudley had been carried off by the gryphon, and Cherice had escaped. The dragons were still captive. What *more* could the dresses want?

"Do you think the dresses are alive?" Roger whispered.

"Yes," I whispered back. "Sort of. They're full of magic, so they *seem* alive."

"So are they or not?" he asked, tucking his cap into his back pocket.

I chewed on my lower lip. I wasn't sure I could explain it. The dresses had a mind of their own; that much was sure. They slept when Lyric wasn't in the closet. And they could be killed. Eighteen was proof of that. I'd left it off its hanger overnight. And though I'd hung it back up as soon as I could, Eighteen no longer woke with the others.

"Can anybody wear the dresses?" Roger asked, distracted by a flapping sleeve.

The sleeve belonged to One, an aqua gown with gold-trimmed sleeves and a full skirt. It waved, straining its seams to catch my attention.

"No," I said, pulling One off its hanger.

I didn't know if this was true. Marci, who used to be the Head Scrubber but now was the Wardrobe Mistress, had worn the dresses when she was a child, but that was *years* ago. As far as I knew, no one else had.

"So there are rules," I went on. "You can wear a dress outside, but not in the rain." I thought about that for a moment. "Or in the snow—they're both wet. You can't leave a dress off its hanger. You have to wear it until you put it back."

"Or what happens?"

I inhaled deeply. "The dress dies."

Roger stared at me as if that were crazy, but I plunged on.

"Let me show you how this works." I slipped my arms into One's sleeves. The dress blurred around me as it snuggled up tight, instantly conforming to my size.

Roger flinched.

"It's still me," I told him, turning around to look in the mirror on the back of the closet door.

A smiling reflection greeted me. A lady with an elaborate hairdo stood in the mirror. I didn't recognize her, but her big diamond brooch told me she was wealthy.

Roger jabbed my shoulder, snatching his finger back as if it had been burned.

"Are you in there?" he whispered.

"It's me, Roger," I said. "Really. Here."

I stuck my hand out. He took it gingerly with two fingers.

"See, it's like a mask. It looks like the lady in the mirror, but it's really me." I squeezed his hand. "Doesn't it feel like me?"

"It does," he said, snatching his hand back. "Wow." He walked around me, studying me from every angle. "You can't tell. It doesn't even sound like you."

"I know."

"Who are you—I mean, who is the lady?"

"I don't know."

"It could be some lady miles and miles away," he said.

I considered that for a minute. "I don't think so. It never has been before."

"Wow," Roger repeated, and turned to rifle through the dresses. "How long have they been here? Where'd they come from? Who made them? A wizard? Are they enchanted—you know, like with a spell? Or a curse? Or—" Roger took a deep breath. "Maybe they're not really dresses. Maybe they're prisoners of a magical war—enchanted prisoners."

I rolled my eyes; he was starting to sound like one of my stories.

He hauled a dress off its hanger.

Beside me, Lyric whistled.

"What are you doing?" I asked.

"If it works for you, it should work for me," Roger said, stepping into the dress.

I held my breath. I'd learned I couldn't wear a dress twice, but I hadn't worn this one yet. My stomach tightened. I'd promised Roger to show him the closet and how the dresses worked, but *sharing* them was different. Weren't these *my* dresses? I'd found them; I'd worn them to save the Princess. Was it fair if Roger was able to wear them too?

5

Roger yanked the dress up and over his arms.

Nothing happened.

The dresses shivered with indignation. I fought the urge to giggle. Freckle-faced, sandy-haired Roger stood with a wave of flounces rippling around his shoulders. His striped shirtsleeves stuck out underneath. His work boots poked out under the trailing skirt.

Roger couldn't wear the dresses. Maybe the magic only worked for girls. Maybe it only worked for me.

I liked that idea. Only I, Darling the Dress Warrior, could wear *these* dresses.

"It's just a stupid dress." He picked at the skirt as if it had lice crawling on it.

"Take it off," I told him. "Like I said, I'm the only one."

"I didn't want to wear it anyway," he said, and dropped the dress, kicking it aside.

"Nobody told you to." I picked the dress up off the carpet.

The badge on the empty hanger read Thirty-Seven. Had Roger ruined it? Could it still be worn? Gnawing my lower lip, I slipped out of One. I hung it back on its hanger, and then I slid into Thirty-Seven. It snapped to my size. A new lady greeted me in the mirror. I sighed with relief.

At least he hadn't accidentally spoiled it for me.

Thirty-Seven simmered with excitement. The flounces

fluttered about my shoulders anxiously. The skirt billowed as if caught by the wind, and the dress pulled me toward the closet door. I took an involuntary step forward.

"Let's go for a walk," I said. Thirty-Seven tingled in agreement.

"Are you sure?" Roger asked. "Who are you now?"

"Lady What's-Her-Name," I said, pointing at the well-dressed lady in the mirror.

Thirty-Seven hauled me forward another step.

"Where would we go?" Roger asked.

"Downstairs. A quick walk just to see what Thirty-Seven wants."

"What could a *dress* want?" He pulled his cap out of his pocket and twisted it in his hands. As if he needed to be sure it was still only a cap.

"That's what we're going to find out," I said.

I opened the closet door and walked out.

"Darling," he called after me, "come back here!"

I ignored him and walked on, dragged along by an insistent Thirty-Seven. I heard the pounding of Roger's boots as he caught up. I smiled. I knew he couldn't resist. And neither could I, Darling Dimple, Intrepid Explorer. I navigated the castle's corridors, drawn forward by Thirty-Seven. The dress was wrought up about something. It would be interesting to see what.

"This is not a good idea," Roger groused in my ear.

"It's no worse than going out on the roof," I said, reminding him of what we'd done last summer.

At that, he fell into step beside me. "Where are you goin'?"

I caught hold of the newel-post on the main staircase to avoid tripping over Thirty-Seven's lunging skirt. A low rumble of conversation rose up from below.

Roger grabbed me by the shoulder.

"Someone will see you," he warned.

"No, Roger," I said. "They won't. They'll see Lady What's-Her-Name."

He frowned suspiciously. I wormed out of his grip and proceeded down the stairs. The sound of voices receded into the distance. Thirty-Seven hurried me after them; Roger dogged my heels.

The main hall flickered in the glow of candlelight. Hundreds of candles sat in sconces, beaming like little stars. It was so pretty. I caught my reflection in a mirror set in an alcove, and stopped to admire myself.

Lady What's-Her-Name had copper curls and blue eyes. Her gown shimmered an orange-red like the flames on the candles. Gold slippers peeked out from her hem. She was quite lovely. I turned my head this way and that, watching her curls bounce. My real hair was like the fluff of a dandelion; it defeated most attempts to tame it. Even now, I could feel my hair ribbon threatening to slide free. I reached up and pulled it out.

"Are you finished?" Roger asked, wiping his forehead with his sleeve. It was the first day of winter; I couldn't imagine how he could be too warm. "Let's find out what the dress wants and go back upstairs."

"In a moment," I said imperiously, waving my hand as I had seen ladies of the court do.

"Is this young man bothering you, Lady Marguerite?" asked a voice as mellow as an oboe.

It was a voice that sent shivers down my spine. Roger froze, freckles on fire. I turned to the slight figure of the Head Housekeeper, Mrs. Pepperwhistle. Roger didn't answer to her—he worked for the Stable Master—but the castle was her domain. She ruled the Upper-servants with her soft voice and her knee-melting sharp glance.

Thirty-Seven fell flat against me as if the wind carrying it had suddenly died. Evidently, it had decided that whatever it wanted could wait.

I smiled what I hoped was a reassuring smile. "Not at all," I said.

"What is a Stable Boy doing here at this hour?" Mrs. Pepperwhistle wondered. Her black eyes measured Roger from head to foot as if she meant to order his coffin.

"He . . . ," I said with a little cough. "He was reporting to me on my horse."

As far as I knew, Lady Marguerite could have ten horses or none at all. I only hoped Mrs. Pepperwhistle didn't have any idea either.

"I'd have thought the Stable Master would be happy to answer your questions," she said, spying the aquamarine hair ribbon in my fist.

Resisting the urge to squirm, I looked her straight in the eye as I slipped the ribbon onto a little table beside me. I stepped away from the table and patted Roger on the shoulder.

"I can't think of another Stable Boy who is a better hand with horses than little Roger here," I said.

"Really?" Mrs. Pepperwhistle said. "Indeed."

Sweat pooled under my arms, no doubt staining my own dress.

"Good servants are priceless, don't you think?" I smiled broadly. "I'm always delighted to discover one in Her Highness's service."

Mrs. Pepperwhistle murmured her agreement and, wishing me a good evening, melted into the shadows. Thirty-Seven danced a jig about my knees.

Roger smacked my arm with his cap.

"Little Roger?" he said.

"I had to say something. I had to sound like Lady Whatever, didn't I?"

Tugging his cap back on his head, he shrugged. "I suppose, but couldn't you think of something else?"

"You didn't say anything to help matters."

"She might come back. We should go," Roger urged.

Thirty-Seven twisted toward the main stair, signaling its agreement with Roger.

"Okay," I said, turning back to retrieve my ribbon, "just a minute."

The tabletop was empty.

"Roger," I said, "did you pick up my ribbon?"

"What would I do that for?" he asked, looking around as if he expected Mrs. Pepperwhistle to reappear at any moment.

I dropped to the floor and felt under the table. I searched the alcove. I made Roger move his feet and pull out his pockets. But the ribbon was gone.

2

The aquamarine ribbon, a gift from Princess Mariposa, was one of only two treasures I owned. The other was the locket, strung on a slender chain, that had been left to me by my long-dead mother. The locket was a family heirloom, a heavy silver oval inscribed with a starburst on one side and the name WRAY on the other. Inside, it was empty. I liked to stay awake at night imagining the treasure that it had once held. Lately, I favored a magical ruby that granted wishes.

This morning I rubbed my locket between my thumb and forefinger, thinking. I had set the ribbon on the table. There was only Roger and me standing there—Mrs. Pepperwhistle had never come near the table. What had happened to the ribbon?

The castle had magic-filled dresses and dragons

chained to the roof—did it have *ghosts*, too? A tremor shook my right knee.

No, I decided. There were no ghosts or specters, and absolutely no phantoms lurking anywhere in the castle. No, absolutely not.

And I didn't intend to start imagining that there were.

I arrived at the wardrobe hall just as Marci walked out of a closet with a cloak over her arm. She'd changed since becoming Wardrobe Mistress. Her hair wreathed her head in a tidy braid. Her second chin had melted away, and her once-round figure had shrunk to a pleasing plumpness. She wore a dark gray wool dress with a stiff white collar that had a mauve silk scarf knotted under it. The wardrobe keys dangled from a silver chatelaine at her belt.

"Good morning, Darling," Marci said.

Lindy, the Head Presser, and Selma, the Head Laundress, stood before the door to the Princess's dressing room. Selma gripped a paper in her red-knuckled hand. She wore the brown dress and canvas apron that the Under-servants wore in the under-cellar. The hem of her skirt was damp, and the soles of her boots bore a permanent crust of soap. She kept her salt-and-pepper hair twisted up on the back of her head, always ready to dive into the job at hand. Selma simmered with energy, like a boiling kettle.

"Good morning," I replied to Marci.

"I'd like to know the meaning of this," Selma said, waving the paper at Lindy.

"I thought I made myself plain. Too much starch in the petticoats," Lindy replied.

"I used the same amount that I've always used, and no one has *ever* complained," Selma said.

"Well, the petticoat this mornin' could have stood guard out in the hall!" Lindy grinned at her own joke.

"You see here," Selma said. "I know my business. If you knew yours, you'd press things up properly and not blame your bad work on others."

"Bad work!" Lindy exclaimed. I could almost see the steam rising off her head.

"Yes, bad work," Selma said, warming to the subject. "Any Presser who knew her business would mind *it* and not mine!"

I slid closer to the pressing room. I worked for Lindy, but I'd known Selma in the under-cellar. Each was convinced that *nobody* worked harder or did a better job than she did. I didn't want to get dragged into the argument and asked to choose sides.

Marci stepped between them.

"Did either of you borrow my scissors?" Marci demanded.

Both shook their heads, momentarily distracted.

"Whyever would I do that?" Selma wondered aloud.

"Several things have gone missing: thread, a pincushion, a pair of scissors," Marci said. "I thought someone had borrowed them and meant to put them back."

"It wasn't me," Selma said, eyeing Lindy.

Lindy's eyes narrowed.

I slipped my hand around the pressing room doorknob.

"Darling," Marci said, "did you borrow my scissors?"

"No, ma'am," I said.

"My best shawl disappeared," Selma said. "And I heard that the Head Footman can't find his nail file."

"Really?" Marci said.

I didn't wait to hear about it. I ducked into the safety of the pressing room. A basket of clean linens sat waiting for me. I shifted my irons onto the stove and picked up a towel.

There on the ironing board lay my aquamarine ribbon.

I stared at it as if it were a poisonous snake. I stepped back, expecting that any minute some ghostly hand would reach out and—

The door opened and Princess Mariposa swept in. The Princess wore her newest winter-weight gown. The wine-colored plaid was nothing like the bright, frothy gowns she'd worn all summer, but it was still beautiful. She toyed with the emerald pin at her collar.

"I am going out," Princess Mariposa said. "I'd like you to accompany me."

I was so surprised that all I could do was nod dumbly.

"Come along, then," she said, going back to the ward-robe hall.

I returned the irons to their stand and eyed the rib-bon. It was real silk, one of the Princess's own that she'd given me. Spooky or not, it was still mine. I snatched it up, stuffed it in my apron pocket, and hurried after her.

By this time, Selma had left and Marci was helping the Princess into a fur-trimmed cloak.

"Ring for Francesca," the Princess said to Lindy.

Lindy hovered by the desk, still red-cheeked from her tussle with Selma. But she went to the thick tapestry bell-pull hanging on the wall and tugged.

I realized that my mouth hung open. I snapped it shut. I was going out with the Princess! Me! Darling Dimple, Under-presser, was accompanying Her Royal Highness!

Francesca appeared in answer to the bell's summons. Her black braids swung with her quick steps. She curt-sied. Her smile suggested that she hoped I was in the sort of trouble that would cause me to be pushed off the tallest tower at daybreak.

"Francesca," the Princess said, "order my coach. See to it that Darling has her coat. Oh, and, Francesca, do not tell *anyone* that I am going."

"Yes, Your Highness." Francesca smiled, but she threw me a suspicious look as she departed.

I twisted my hands together. I was going out with the Princess! But where?

Marci knelt down to help the Princess out of her slippers and into her boots.

When Princess Mariposa was ready, she turned to me. "Have you ever visited the Royal Cemetery?" she asked.

I shook my head.

"Then it's about time you did," she replied.

3

I trotted along as Princess Mariposa hurried down the stairs to the main hall. She'd told Francesca to get my coat, but I didn't have a coat. My old coat had become too tight and too short, and Jane had given it away. One of the Seamstresses meant to use it to make slippers. Once she cut away all the frayed and holey parts, there would be just enough fabric left over.

I glanced up at the Princess. I'd seen her appear thoughtful, sad, wounded, and even—one time—horrified, but I'd never seen the expression she wore now. It was a look I'd once seen on Jane's face—a sort of longing, as if there was something missing that she couldn't find.

What could Princess Mariposa long for that she couldn't get? She had everything: gowns, jewels, a castle—

a whole kingdom! If the Princess was searching for something, maybe she hadn't looked in the right place yet.

But whatever it was, I doubted she would find it in the Royal Cemetery.

Francesca was waiting at the front doors with a coat over her arm when we arrived. If I hadn't known that she'd taken a shortcut down the back stairs, I'd have been impressed. The Princess drifted off to gaze out the tall front windows as Francesca helped me into the coat, a dark silver wool with a velvet collar and cuffs. I buttoned the fat pewter buttons down the front and smoothed the soft cuffs. Francesca rolled her eyes. *She* was used to fine clothes, but I wasn't. I sighed at the thought of returning the coat to her later, when I noticed the word *Darling* embroidered in silver thread on the cuff.

This was my coat!

"Mine," I breathed.

"Don't be a ninny," Francesca whispered.

"Just in time, my dear," called Lady Kaye, the Baroness Azure. She crossed the room, rapping the floor with her silver-capped cane. She had her other arm hooked through Prince Sterling's, pulling him along beside her.

Princess Mariposa arched an eyebrow at Francesca.

"I didn't tell anyone," Francesca protested.

"I knew you'd want to pay your respects, and I knew

you'd want my company," Lady Kaye said, releasing the Prince's arm. "And dear Sterling offered to escort us both!"

This smelled a little fishy to me, and from the wrinkling of the Princess's nose, I could tell it smelled to her, too. But she smiled and thanked them for their thoughtfulness.

"Let's be off, then," the Baroness commanded as if she were the Princess. The Guards hastened to throw open the doors for her as she sailed through, cane aloft.

Princess Mariposa followed, biting her lower lip. Prince Sterling winked at me and offered me his arm. The Prince, whose full name was Humphrey Frederic Albert Sterling, insisted that he preferred Sterling. That was a good thing, since we'd all known him as that before we knew his full name. We were used to it. And I thought Sterling a much grander name than Humphrey.

"Nice coat," he said as we walked outdoors.

"It's new," I told him, unable to resist.

"Very becoming."

I beamed. I was glad he'd decided to stay for the winter—some business about waiting for a ship's arrival. The other servants doubted this reason, but it sounded fine to me. I didn't want him to go home to Tamzin.

The coach gleamed with gold fittings. A team of great white horses stamped their hooves in the cold. The scent of snow filled the air. A rim of frost clung to the coach wheels—which stood as high as my shoulder! The Baroness and the Princess were already bundled up under a fur coverlet when a Footman helped me climb the steps and slip inside the coach. I settled on a velvet-upholstered seat and pressed my nose to the frosty little window at my side. The curve in the glass distorted my view so that now the front of the castle stretched up into the sky like a glistening white candle.

The seat bounced slightly as Prince Sterling settled in beside me. The Footman tucked a fur coverlet around us. Then he saluted and snapped the coach door shut. A whip cracked above and we were off. The *clop-clop* of the horses' hooves on the stone pavement echoed in the crisp air. Excitement buzzed in my veins. I was riding in a coach pulled by six white horses, and anything could happen. Why, any minute now they might leap off the pavement and fly through the pale sky, up, *up*—

"Now, my dear, you mustn't be cross with me. I do like a nice stroll through the Royal Cemetery. So many old friends to visit there," Lady Kaye said in a voice intended to sound soothing. "Including your dear, dear parents."

Princess Mariposa's breath stirred the fur around her hood. "I understand, but I prefer to visit my parents' graves alone and—"

"Then why did you bring Darling along?" Lady Kaye interrupted.

Startled, the Princess turned to her.

21

"Because I'm sure she'd like to visit her parents' graves."

Lady Kaye pinked slightly at this and raised an eyebrow. A long silence followed as the two women, the powerful Baroness and her ruler, stared each other down. I sucked in my breath, trying to predict who would blink first.

"Are your parents buried in the Royal Cemetery?" Prince Sterling asked.

"I don't know. My father was lost at sea," I began. "Captain James Fortune—"

"That's a good name. Why don't you use it?" Prince Sterling asked.

I hadn't thought about it before. Jane had slapped the name Dimple on me the day I was born. It had been mine for so long that it felt cozy, like a pair of warm socks. But Fortune was my real last name.

"I guess I should," I said, trying to imagine the name Darling Fortune tripping off my tongue.

"Men lost at sea aren't buried in cemeteries," Lady Kaye said.

"But my mother could be," I said. "She was an Underchopper."

Lady Kaye blinked at that.

"Few servants are buried in the Royal Cemetery," she admonished me. "Who was your mother?"

"Emily Wray, um, Fortune. Emily Wray Fortune," I replied.

"Her mother was a *Wray*?" Lady Kaye spoke as if this were nonsense.

"According to Marci," Princess Mariposa said.

I unbuttoned my top coat button and pulled my locket out for her to see.

The Baroness leaned forward and stared.

"I don't believe it!" she announced.

"Well, it appears she was," Princess Mariposa said, hiding her smile behind her glove. "All the Wrays are buried in the Royal Cemetery," she said to me. "I'll instruct the Warden to help you locate them."

Lady Kaye settled back into the seat cushions with a *sniff*.

"Thank you, Your Highness," I replied.

We'd left the castle grounds behind and were dashing down the mountain road to the city. A fairyland of silver-and-white-laced trees danced past. The sound of adult talk blended in with the *clip-clop* of the horses' hooves. I sank into a reverie of fairies and frost minions battling it out over who would rule the forest. Before I knew it, the forest had melted into farms and households and then into the city itself.

I'd been to the city twice, but not since Jane's eyesight

had grown so bad. Jane had raised me; I had followed her around the castle kitchens until she'd become too near-sighted to work as an Under-slicer. Now she worked with the Pickers. I still saw her regularly, but I had my own job.

The city was even bigger and more exciting than I remembered. Houses, parks, tree-lined avenues, shops and buildings, and more shops and houses whirled past in wavy lines through the window. People on doorsteps waved as the coach passed by.

I pressed my nose against the glass so that they could better see me, Darling Dimp—*Fortune,* riding in the royal carriage. Just like a real princess. I smoothed the skirt of my brand-new coat and imagined it was the finest gown ever sewn.

"You're marking up the glass," Prince Sterling whispered.

I jerked back from the window as we passed under a heavy wrought-iron arch and into the Royal Cemetery. I rubbed at the glass with my coat sleeve while the coach rounded to a stop. The Footman helped us out, starting with the Princess. I stared all around, blinking in the sudden sunshine.

The Royal Cemetery was a park! Frost-trimmed lawns stair-stepped up a hill covered in trees and hedges and skirted by little stone paths. Pretty statues and empty flower boxes dotted the landscape. Squinting in surprise,

I noticed the tidy graves tucked in among it all, spoiling the effect.

A short, stout, white-whiskered man dressed in a heavy canvas apron over a black overcoat came jogging toward us, pulling off a pair of gardening gloves. His feet were so small that his whole body jiggled with each step.

"Good day! Good day!" he cried. "Welcome! Beautiful day, Your Highness, yes indeed! A beautiful day to visit this place of peace." He bowed so low that he wobbled on his tiny feet.

I tensed, worried that he'd fall over. The Princess reached out as if she had the same concern.

"Good morning, Warden Graves," Princess Mariposa said, hand in midair.

I giggled; Prince Sterling nudged me. I glanced up, expecting to be scolded, but he grinned. His warm brown eyes flashed.

"Interesting name," he whispered.

I nodded.

At that moment, the Warden's head popped up. Spying the Princess's outstretched hand, he beamed. He grabbed the hand and kissed her glove with a loud *smack*.

"At your service!" Warden Graves said. "Shall I escort you to the Royal Tomb?"

Princess Mariposa shook her head. "I prefer to go alone."

Warden Graves's smile faded. "Of course," he said,

nodding. He tucked his gloves under his arm and fished in the pockets of his overcoat. "I have the keys. I do." His fist came out of his pocket with a *pop*. A set of gold keys dangled from his fingers. He laid them in the Princess's hands gently, as if they were made of glass. "Sound the gong if you require anything, Your Majesty, and I shall come at once."

"Thank you," she replied with a sad smile, and set off, vanishing into the shrubbery beyond. She'd forgotten all about me.

I twisted one of the fat buttons on my coat, wondering what I should do.

The Baroness tapped her cane on the turf. "There's nothing worse than wallowing," she said.

"Except impatience," Prince Sterling said under his breath.

"Or mumbling," she snapped.

The Warden stepped from foot to foot as if unsure of his balance. "Perhaps, Your Grace, I could offer myself as an escort?"

Lady Kaye looked down her long nose at the little man. "Prince Sterling is my escort," she replied, as if this were obvious.

"Thank you, Warden, for your offer," Prince Sterling said, squeezing my shoulder. "This young lady would like to make use of it."

The Prince winked at me as he took Lady Kaye's arm and they ambled off.

That left me, Darling Fortune, all alone in the cemetery with Warden Graves. My heart pounded. I'd never been to a cemetery before, and the thought of all those dead folks left me shaky. The sun slid behind a cloud. Gray shadows hovered over the stark, leafless trees and stone paths. The wind moaned. An icy chill stung my cheeks. I bit my lip; was that a ghost lurking behind that pillar?

"Of what service may I be?" the Warden asked.

I found myself looking into his twinkling blue eyes. He smiled as if he couldn't wait to show off his cemetery to someone. I cleared my throat. Maybe this was my chance to learn something about my mother.

"I think my mother might be buried here. Her name was Emily Wray Fortune."

"Emily Wray! Of course. I remember her. Pretty girl," he said, rocking on his heels. "Terrible tragedy, that. She died so young."

"Was she pretty?" I asked, surprised.

"Very pretty. Much like you—fair, with beautiful blond hair."

"Oh."

"The Wrays are in the older section," Warden Graves said, and, taking my elbow, led me down a broad path.

We walked between carved tombstones that proclaimed this or that beloved person was buried there. The Warden pointed out unusual mausoleums and told me entertaining facts about the occupants. *The dear departed,* he called them, as if he'd known them all personally. Maybe he had; he looked old enough to me.

Gradually, the stones grew smaller and closer together until we passed through a thicket of tombstones lined up like soldiers on parade. Here, uneven tiles paved the walkway. Great oaks towered overhead, casting long, dark shadows. Gravestones gleamed from between their roots like broken teeth.

A sharp wind tugged at my coat. I kept a tight grip on the Warden's arm; this was one place I did not want to get lost.

The path ended at a black gate with the name *Wray* curled in black metal letters over the top. Two black angels stood guard on either side, holding torches aloft. Their marble faces glowered at me. The Wrays had their own private little cemetery. And from the look of their guardian angels, they didn't want anyone going in there.

"Here we are! Of course, long ago the torches would have been lit anytime the family visited. . . ." The Warden gave an embarrassed chuckle.

"Is it locked?" I whispered, not at all sure I wanted the gate opened.

"Locked?" The Warden coughed. "I don't think so. It never used to be."

He walked over to the gate and gave it a push. It groaned but refused to budge. The Warden yanked on his gloves, took hold of the gate with both hands, and shoved. The hinges shrieked like a scalded kitchen maid as the gate lunged open. The Warden tumbled forward, catching himself to avoid toppling into the shadowy space beyond. He steadied himself and favored me with an unconvincing smile.

"Not locked," he said. "See."

I peered inside. Frost iced the ground and the trees with a ghostly glaze. Dead leaves brooded in clumps between the stones. Shadowy statues lurked in the distance. Mist rolled down the frosted path, as if something suddenly awakened by the screech of the gate's opening was coming to investigate. I took a step backward.

"The Wrays were a great house once, rich and powerful. The tombs are some of the most elaborate in the cemetery," the Warden said in a hushed, almost reverent voice.

"What happened?"

He licked his lip, considering. "They made bad choices, I suppose."

"Bad choices?"

"I make it a rule never to speak ill of the dead," he said. "May they rest in peace."

"Wh-where is my mother?" I asked, hating to think of her somewhere in that gloomy place.

At that, the Warden snapped his fingers. "This way."

I went with him through the gate, hunching my shoulders. I hoped the Wrays didn't mind my coming, seeing how rich and powerful they'd been and seeing how poor and unimportant I was. I found myself clutching the locket, ready to thrust it out at any specter who challenged my right to be there.

The mist gave way to marble arches and pillars, to great statues of men seated on horses. Some tombs were carved all over with leaves and flowers. Some still held traces of gold and silver where they'd once been decorated. *Vespera Wray,* one proclaimed in rose-colored granite. *Barnett Wray! Ramira! Xavier! Lorette!* the names of the Wrays screamed from their stones.

And then they grew small and quiet, simple little stones with names obscured by weeds. Something had silenced the Wrays. I wondered what it was.

"Over here," the Warden said, pointing to a little stone set in a cramped corner.

Emily Wray Fortune, her pale gray stone whispered in tiny letters.

"I found a spot for her," the Warden said, drawing a handkerchief out of his pocket and cleaning off her stone. "She was the last of the Wrays."

The last of the Wrays echoed in the stillness.

"The last one?" I asked.

"The very last," he replied. "You must understand, my dear, that there wasn't room for your father here."

"He was lost at sea," I said.

"Of course! Silly me," Warden Graves exploded, and rambled on about what a tragedy it all was.

I nodded, only half paying attention. All these rich and powerful Wrays—and my poor mother, who had worked in the castle kitchens, was the very last one. I squeezed her locket, the last thing left by the Wrays. And now it belonged to me.

"I didn't think *he'd* mind," the Warden added.

"Who?" I asked, my spine tingling so that I glanced over my shoulder for *him.*

The Warden waved at the stone behind my mother's, a dull gray marble column that tapered to a jagged point at the top. Moss had ensnared it, obscuring most of the bottom half. A gilded fence encompassed its base. Dead roses peeked between the narrow, barbed posts. Overhanging branches raked the top of the stone, which blended into the wall behind it.

I hadn't noticed it before.

"I usually trim them back each fall, but . . ." The Warden waved a glove at the roses. "This past fall, the wedding . . . I mean, when we didn't have the wedding." He reddened.

I leaned over my mother's stone to the pillar. I curled my fingers in the moss and yanked. Dried-up vegetation crumbled in my hand. Underneath, the carving of a starburst appeared.

I gripped my locket, holding it up to the stone. It was the same design.

The very same. The same starburst that sat at the only spot on the castle grounds where you could stand and see the dragons on the castle roof!

My pulse pounded in my ears. I scrambled to scratch more of the dead moss from the stone. And there, under the starburst, silver letters gleamed in the dull morning.

MAGNIFICENT WRAY

ARCHITECT

"Magnificent Wray?" I asked.

"The greatest Wray of all. The King's Architect," the Warden replied.

My mother, the Under-chopper, was tucked at the foot of greatness. I hoped Magnificent wasn't disappointed.

"Which king?" I asked, although I already knew in my heart which one.

"King Richard."

Princess Mariposa's grandfather, who had collared the dragons and built the castle.

"I suppose Magnificent Wray would be your great-great-grandfather, young lady," the Warden said. "How about that?"

The letters winked at me as a shaft of sunlight pierced the gloom. *Your great-great-grandfather,* the wind murmured.

"What's an architect?"

Warden Graves chuckled. "Someone who builds buildings."

"What kind of buildings?"

"All kinds. The cathedral in town, the big one with the maritime chapel—your father would be memorialized there. All the sailors lost at sea are, you know."

"Huh." I rubbed the surface of the letters with my thumb.

"And the Star Castle is probably his most magnificent accomplishment. Ha-ha, *magnificent*—a little pun there."

"Princess Mariposa's castle?"

"The very same."

My heart thudded. Magnificent Wray had built the castle for King Richard—with the dragons! The very castle I lived in! The castle that hummed with magic. I traced each letter in the word *architect,* feeling for the pulse of the magic. And finding nothing.

Below the letters, something glistened through the remaining moss. I brushed the moss away, and words carved in gold glimmered at me.

Light shines, I read.

Light shines? Every other gravestone said something like *Rest in peace* or *Beloved mother and father* or *In loving memory.* That made sense. That's what I would put on a gravestone. Not *Light shines.* What did light have to do with a creepy place guarded by black angels?

4

By the time I got back, lunch was past and my work waited for me. Lindy had left me a tray and a note: *Gone out. I want this all done by dinnertime! Lindy.* Off to visit her beau, the Captain of the Guard, I assumed. I gobbled down my food, tied my hair back with my ribbon, and got to work.

My brain buzzed like a hive full of angry bees. Questions multiplied like unwashed pots on a feast day. What had happened to the Wrays? How could they have been so rich and my mother so poor? The Warden had said that Magnificent Wray was the greatest Wray, but his tombstone was much smaller than the older ones. What made him so great? What on earth was *Light shines* supposed to mean? How had my mother felt about being the last of the Wrays?

The very notion of being the last Wray sent a shiver down my spine.

By the time I folded the final sheet, it was dark outside. I tidied myself up and set off. The glow from the hearth's embers lit the faces of the Under-servants clustered in the castle kitchens. Some of them polished boots, sewed, or whittled to keep their hands busy. But their real reason for gathering was to talk.

The Head Cook had her own domain, a corner with a desk and a towering bookcase crammed full of recipe books. She perched on a high stool, squinting at papers, choosing the occasional nut from a bowl at her elbow. She scrutinized each one before popping it into her mouth as if every bite had to meet her standards.

I leaned against her desk and waited for her to notice me.

"Five, but I thought there were six," she muttered, tapping the paper in her hand and crunching a nut.

"Six what?" I said.

"Six dozen eggs," she said, raising an eyebrow. "To what do I owe the pleasure of your company?"

I shrugged. "Thought I'd say hello."

"Hello," she said.

"Six dozen eggs doesn't seem like that many for all of us," I commented.

"Goodness, no. We use many, many more than that in a day. These were put aside in my cupboard."

"For what?"

"A new recipe I want to try," she replied, shuffling through her papers. "A meringue, it's called. It's made out of lots of egg whites. It's supposed to look like an edible cloud."

"Sounds pretty but not very tasty." Although at that moment, I'd have eaten almost anything.

"Well, it's sweetened with sugar and topped with raspberries."

My stomach chose that moment to gurgle like an emptying sink.

"Did you miss supper?" the Head Cook inquired.

Every servant knew that mealtimes were sacred. Miss a meal and you went hungry. But. I'd learned long ago that the Head Cook had a soft spot for starving children.

"It was my fault," I said. "I was so long finishing my work."

"Why was that?" she asked, putting her papers down.

"I had to go out with the Princess all morning, so I started late."

The Head Cook tucked a stray hair back into her bun. "All morning?" she asked.

I nodded. "We went to the Royal Cemetery."

She snorted. "Of all places to drag a child! Tilly!" she barked over her shoulder. "Fetch a bowl of leftover stew and round up a crust of bread."

"Thank you," I said sincerely.

She held out her bowl. "Have a nut."

"Thank you." I selected a plump one.

A harried-looking Kitchen Maid appeared with a bowl of stew and a slab of bread drizzled with honey. I thanked her. She eyed me like a rat in the pantry, but I ignored her and scampered off to a safe corner to eat. When I'd finished every drop and eaten every crumb, licking the last trace of honey off my fingers, I glanced around.

I had questions. Someone had to know something. Who?

The Head Cook had a pencil between her teeth and a paper clutched in her fist. She might know more than the others, but she didn't appear as if she wanted to be interrupted again. My gaze drifted over the Under-servants. Roger perched on a hearthstone, whittling. He looked like he'd recovered from his encounter with Mrs. Pepperwhistle. But he was as short on answers as I was. I'd talk to him later.

I spotted Jane on a bench next to a table where Marci sat sewing. Jane hoarded secrets like a squirrel guarding nuts. *She* had answers—if not about the Wrays, then about my mother.

I squeezed into the knot of servants and wiggled my way onto the bench.

"That Sterling fellow keeps hanging around," one of them grumbled. "All the other guests had sense enough to leave after the wedding fell apart."

"He's sweet on Her Highness," a Kitchen Maid said with a giggle.

"Well, she ain't sweet on him," a Cook retorted. "He's a third son!"

"Second," Marci corrected, sewing a button on a sleeve. She belonged with the Upper-servants now, but she still spent time in the kitchens. "And it's just as well. If she married an heir to another throne, where would they live? He might take her to his kingdom and leave us stuck with a regent."

"The castle wouldn't be the same without Her Highness," a Groom said.

The group sighed glumly.

I'd listened to their chatter my whole life without minding, but tonight I squirmed impatiently. I needed answers, and all they wanted to talk about was the Princess getting married.

I slid closer to Jane. She was knitting me winter socks. I'd chosen the yarn. She could knit by feel, but choosing colors was another story. Not that she couldn't see, but she was so shortsighted that she mistook similar colors for each other. If I didn't pick out three balls of yarn that were identical, I was apt to end up with stripy socks. To Jane, red and bright pink were the same, and lilac and gray looked alike.

"Thank you for knitting me socks," I began.

"You are welcome," Jane told me.

"I was thinking about my mother," I began.

"She was a sweet, kind person and a dear friend," Jane said, stopping to count her stitches.

That's what she always said.

"I know, but—" I said.

Gillian, the Under-dryer, appeared from nowhere and plopped herself next to me on the bench. She waved a paper-wrapped piece of toffee under my nose.

"Are you thinking up a story?" she asked, her eyes bright and her dark curls kinked with excitement.

I eyed the candy; I'd appreciated the stew and the bread, but it hadn't filled me up entirely. I still had room for a slice of pie, a piece of cake—or several dozen toffees. But the hive of angry questions in my brain buzzed louder than my hunger.

"I don't have one now, but I will later," I offered.

Gillian sighed dramatically, and the toffee disappeared into her bulging apron pocket. Then she flopped back on the bench as if she'd never hear another story.

"I heard that Prince Sterling went with Her Highness

today in the royal carriage," Esperanza, the Head Icer, piped up. "And Darling went with them."

"Darling?" a Gardener exclaimed.

They all turned to stare at me.

"That Darling," one of them said. "She's up there all day hearing what goes on, but does she ever tell us anything?"

A spark flew up from the embers and drifted on the air. Someone dropped a thimble that went clattering across the flagstones. But their eyes stayed on me.

"Well ...," I said. I didn't like to talk about the Princess. She was the *Princess*, after all, not some Sweeper. But the pointed looks on their faces told me I wasn't wriggling out of it this time. I sighed. Questioning Jane would have to wait.

"Prince Sterling did go along," I admitted. They could find that much out from the Footmen.

"Ooooh," one of them breathed. "They went together?"

I shook my head. "Only in the carriage. At the cemetery, the Princess went off by herself, and the Prince escorted the Baroness; she said she had old friends to visit."

"What did you do?" Gillian asked, popping back up, eyes alight. "Chase ghosts? Open a hidden vault and find—"

"If you'd let her answer, you'd find out," Marci said.

A coal of inspiration sparked in me. Here was the perfect opportunity to dangle the Wrays in front of the

Under-servants. Maybe I wouldn't have to pry things out of Jane after all.

"Warden Graves—" I began, stopping when an outburst of laughter interrupted me. "He can't help his name!" I exclaimed. Names were a sensitive subject to me. Anyone named Darling would understand.

"Go on," Marci said.

"Warden Graves showed me my mother's grave," I finished. "It—"

"Poor little Emily," the Soup Chef moaned.

All the older servants *tsk-tsk*ed.

"Was it a nice stone?" one asked.

"Yes, it was nice," I said. "She's next to a big monument and—"

"She was a sweet girl," one of the Laundresses mused. "If only she hadn't fallen for that good-for-nothing sailor."

My ears perked up. Father was a good-for-nothing? What?

"That's enough," Jane barked, reddening. "Darling had a sad day. I'm sure it was kind of the Princess to take her, but enough is enough. And leave Emily alone! She's not here to defend herself."

"That's right," one of the Grooms said. "Don't talk bad about the dead."

I shriveled like one of Magnificent Wray's dead roses. Trust Jane to stick up for me just when I didn't want her to.

"Hmm," Marci said, eyeing Jane. "So, Darling, it was a nice stone?"

I wanted to hug her. I didn't, of course, but right then I could have.

"Yes. Right next to Magnificent Wray," I announced, glancing around.

The younger servants' faces stayed blank, but the older ones' shone with awe. Servants from nearby clusters looked up when the name was mentioned. Several drifted closer to our group.

"Magnificent Wray," a nearly bald Picker named Agnes echoed. "Oh my."

"Did you know him?" I asked, hanging on the edge of the bench.

"Don't be ridiculous," Agnes snapped.

"He died a long, long time ago," Marci said, selecting another button from her sewing box.

"He was an old man when King Richard was crowned," the Head Cook agreed, looking up from her papers. "Think how long ago *that* was."

"Sorry," I mumbled.

"My grandmother, who was a little girl when the castle was built, probably could tell you a story or two if she were here," Marci said.

"So could the Librarian," the Soup Chef added.

"That old windbag," the Pastry Chef said with a laugh.

"Windbag?" a Scrubber groused. "Doesn't say two words to anybody, doesn't leave his library. Windbag indeed!"

"Maybe he only talks to people worth talking to," the Pastry Chef said.

The Scrubber jumped out of her seat, banging into the copper pans above her. "I know when I've been insulted!" she cried, rubbing her forehead.

"Oh, sit down," the Head Cook said. "All the Upperservants have their airs."

Marci sniffed.

"Well, all the ones who think their jobs are more important than everyone else's," the Head Cook amended. "So, Marci, do you think the Princess is interested in this Sterling?"

"Hmm," Marci said through her teeth, snapping off a thread. "She likes him, but will she risk her heart a second time?"

"Oh, her poor bruised heart," one of the Sweepers groaned, pressing her hands to her chest.

"Princess Mariposa has been *so* sad," the Head Cook agreed. "Not even my best soufflé cheered her up."

"She needs time for her heart to mend," an Underduster chimed in.

"Bosh," the Scrubber grumbled, still massaging her head. "I say one prince is as good as another."

"She can't marry just anyone," Marci disagreed.

"Well," the Pastry Chef exclaimed, "let's hurry and *pick* someone for her!"

And with that, they were once again absorbed in their favorite subject, the Princess's love life. I sank back against the bench, rubbing my locket between my fingers. I polished *Wray* with my thumb. I'd be Jane's age before I pieced together any information from the Under-servants.

But the Librarian sounded promising.

5

Roger hooked me by the arm outside the kitchens as I headed back upstairs.

"What?" I asked, my voice echoing down the empty corridor.

I'd sat by the fire thinking until late. With winter, darkness came early and the cold wormed its way into the castle through every crevice it could find. Most of the Under-servants were already tucked beneath layers of quilts for the night. Candles flickered in sconces along the dark walls, casting dancing shadows across the flagstones.

"How'd you get it back?" Roger asked. "Were you foolin' with me?"

I shrugged. "Get what back?"

"Your ribbon."

I reached up to touch my aquamarine ribbon, remembering.

"No, it was gone. But then this morning, it was lying on my ironing board."

Roger glanced over his shoulder, considering. "Who put it there?"

"An Upper-duster, maybe."

"How'd they know whose ribbon it was?"

"A good guess?"

He licked his lip, brow furrowed. "Doesn't seem likely."

It didn't. A stray ribbon in a castle this big, with this many people . . . I hadn't even lost it anywhere near where I was *supposed* to be.

"One thing's for sure," Roger said, lowering his voice. "It wasn't a ghost."

"No," I agreed fervently. "It couldn't have been."

" 'Cause there ain't such things as ghosts," he added.

We stood there in the ghost-free corridor, staring at each other.

"I could walk you upstairs," Roger offered, twisting his cap on his head.

I thought about the miles of empty, silent corridors between me and the Girls' dormitory. For a moment, I was tempted. Not that I was scared, but only because Roger seemed so concerned.

Just then, I caught a glimmer of something out of the

corner of my eye—a shifting bit of icy whiteness in the shadows. It seemed to flow out of a doorway and toward the far end of the hall. Goose bumps rose on my arms.

Roger's eyes widened; his freckles bleached away. "Did you see that?" he whispered.

"See what?" I said, hoping he hadn't seen what I'd seen.

Down the corridor, a faint creak sounded.

"Did you hear that?" Roger asked.

I nodded, unable to speak. My tongue was glued to the roof of my mouth.

I grabbed Roger's arm. We pivoted to peer behind us. A glimmer of white coasted into the deep darkness at the end of the hallway. Then—as if someone blew out a match—it vanished.

"Should we go check?" Roger asked.

Of all the dumb ideas he'd ever had, that was the dumbest. But then he started off down the corridor without waiting for me to reply. Which meant I had to either stand there all by myself with who-knows-what lurking who-knows-where or run after him.

So I grabbed a candle out of its sconce and pelted down the hall. The darkness raced ahead of my tiny circle of candlelight. My heart galloped right along with it, pumping like a Kitchen Maid fetching water.

Roger stood at a dead-end wall, running his hands over the panels.

"It went right through here."

I held the candle close to the panel. The scent of lemon wood polish tickled my nose. But all I could see was an ordinary wall.

"It went right through it," Roger said. "Like it wasn't even there."

My eye twitched. My knee trembled. I held on to my candle as if it were the only solid thing in the castle. You could climb out on the roof and reassure yourself that the dragons were still there, hardened to stone and nicely chained down. Ghosts were a different matter.

You couldn't exactly tie one up or lock it in a cupboard.

"The castle is haunted," Roger breathed, his brown eyes aglow.

"Don't be ridiculous," I said, loud enough for any phantom to hear. "There's no such things as ghosts."

Ghosts, the corridor echoed in response.

6

The echo stayed with me as I cowered under my covers, willing myself to go to sleep. But all thoughts of ghosts melted away in the morning light. My hair crackled with static electricity. My hairbrush felt solid in my grip. The mirror held only my reflection. Not a spectral shadow was in sight.

Did I really look like my mother? I wondered, studying my pale, snub-nosed face. Warden Graves had said so. He'd said she was fair, like me. I batted my pale lashes, watching the light reflect in my almost-aquamarine eyes.

"Here," Francesca said, thrusting a dress under my nose.

I took the gray wool dress in my hands, marveling at its softness. Around the Girls' dormitory, the other Princess's Girls were pulling on their new dresses.

"I hate wool dresses," the smallest Girl said. "They itch."

"Here, Dulcie," one of the others called, tossing her something. "Try wearing a petticoat for once."

The room exploded in giggles. Dulcie turned crimson, twisting the petticoat in her hands. At nine, she was the youngest Girl. She dashed around, braids flying, fetching and carrying, quicker than any of the other Girls. She was Francesca's favorite when it came to running messages around the castle. *But.* She hated wearing her apron. Hated braiding her long red hair. Hated washing before bedtime. And most of all, hated wearing petticoats, which she claimed slowed her down.

"Don't forget your camisole," another said.

"Or your long stockings," a third added.

The flush on Dulcie's face crept down her cheeks and across her neck. She yanked on her clothes, muttering under her breath.

"Stupid, stupid clothes," I heard her say.

I slid into the new dress, settling it over my petticoat. It was a shade darker than the silver-gray fall dress I'd been wearing, and different in style. The fall dresses were cut from a heavier cotton than the summer dresses and had three-quarter-length sleeves. This dress had a stand-up collar and long sleeves with an edging of lace at the wrist. I'd never owned anything with lace on it before. I admired myself in the mirror as I tied on my crisp white apron with the silver butterfly embroidered on the pocket.

"At least Dulcie isn't like Darling!" the oldest, Ann, exclaimed. "Mirror, mirror, on the wall, who's the vainest of us all?"

They howled with laughter.

"You should have seen her yesterday with her coat," Francesca sputtered between fits.

"Don't they wear coats in the under-cellar?" Kate, the tallest, asked.

"Don't need them down there," another Girl answered. "It's too damp and smoky."

"I wonder, Darling, did you have your own pet rat down below?" Ann asked.

I twirled around, letting my petticoat flare the skirt of my new dress.

"I can get you one," I told Ann. "A nice, plump, greasy-tailed friend. Just say the word."

"Oh," Kate cried, jumping on her bed. "You wouldn't!"

"My mother does not allow vermin in the castle," Francesca thundered. "Now get dressed and look sharp."

I grinned at the thought of Mrs. Pepperwhistle menaced by rats.

"Did you see the Princess's new plaid dress?" one of the Girls asked.

"Oooh, it was so pretty," another replied.

"That silk came all the way from Tamzin!" a third exclaimed.

They would prattle on until Francesca sent them packing. I, Darling Fortune, Under-presser, had more important matters to pursue. Magnificent Wray, for one. His starburst was on the castle terrace, my locket, and his gravestone. That had to mean something.

I reached for my locket, which was hanging from my bedpost, and spied two tiny black eyes staring at me from behind my pillow. *Iago.* He and his family lived under my bed in a wooden crate stamped ARTICHOKES. His whiskers grazed the top of my pillow as he blinked twice; he wanted to talk to me. I held up a finger to tell him to wait a minute. Then I took my time putting on my locket and selecting a roll off the breakfast tray. I loitered, nibbling on my roll while the other Girls hurried out of the room.

"Don't be all day," Francesca called over her shoulder as she left.

The moment the door closed, Iago bounced up on the pillow. I crouched down to whisker level.

"Still keeping watch over those dragons?" I asked.

Iago straightened up, tail stiff. He nodded sharply. He was on guard.

It was a good thing. Not that the dragons were apt to go anywhere. They were fettered by magic collars and chained to the castle's tallest spire—not to mention hardened to stone—but, still, they were aware and watching. Iago was my eyes and ears as far as the dragons were concerned. He could scurry up to the roof to check on them. I couldn't; I didn't have the key.

"Good," I told him. "I'll see if I can save some cheese out of my supper."

His tiny black eyes twinkled. His whiskers twitched. I could tell he was pleased.

"Iago," I said, "did you take my ribbon?"

He stared pointedly at my head.

"Yes, I have it now, but I lost it downstairs. Then yesterday morning, I found it on my ironing board. Did you find it and put it there?"

He shook his head.

"Oh," I replied. Thinking that in his scurrying about he might have seen who'd returned the ribbon, I asked, "Do you know who did?"

He shook his whole body violently and tumbled off the pillow onto the eiderdown.

"Someone did." I stood up; it was getting late, and I'd soon be missed.

Iago wrinkled his tiny white forehead.

"Good day," I said. "Stay sharp."

I waved to him as I left. A gnawing uncertainty filled me. Who had taken my ribbon? And who had put it back?

When I walked into the wardrobe hall, Marci pounced on me.

"Lindy burned herself; I need you immediately," she said, rushing me into the pressing room.

"Oh, no, is she hurt?"

"Her arm. I sent her to Pepperwhistle to have it dressed. Meanwhile, you'll have to iron that," she said, pointing to the dress draped over Lindy's ironing board.

One of the Princess's dresses.

"Oh my," I said.

"There isn't time to waste—Her Highness is waiting." Marci shook my shoulder.

"But I've never pressed anything like that."

"I know. I laid it over a chair, and the Baroness sat on it. The sleeve is creased. Just touch it up."

I hesitated, twisting my fingers together.

"I'd do it myself, but I've never ironed," Marci admitted.

I walked over to the dress. It was a heavy emerald silk with an elaborate trim of black velvet ribbons. They traced the bodice down to a sharp point at the waist, like a fan. They edged the sleeves and scrolled across the bottom of the skirt, which flared out in a long train.

"It's awfully fancy," I mumbled.

"It's a court dress."

In the winter, Princess Mariposa met with counselors and advisors, attending to the business of the kingdom. One day a week she sat on her throne and heard petitions from her subjects.

Marci patted my arm. "You can do this. Just avoid the ribbons."

I nodded. You couldn't press velvet; it would squash flat and turn shiny. I took a deep breath. When Lindy had to iron touchy dresses, she used a series of what she called hams and rolls—linen shapes stuffed with sawdust that kept clothes rounded while she worked on them. I selected an arm roll and slid it inside the heavy sleeve. Then, wetting my lower lip with my tongue, I picked up Lindy's iron and *kissed* the surface of the silk with the tip of it.

The crease melted away.

"Perfect," Marci said.

I set the iron down and slipped the arm roll out. Marci gathered up the dress, holding it across her arms like a baby.

"Come with me," she said, turning on her heel.

I walked after her—straight into the Princess's lavender-and-gold dressing room. The Princess stood before her tall mirror, dressed in thick petticoats and a lace-trimmed camisole, reading a letter. Lady Kaye, the Baroness Azure, sat on one of the plush chairs with her fist wrapped around her silver-capped cane. Her dark hair, piled high and glinting with diamond pins, shone with streaks of the same silver as the knob on her cane.

"Well, my dear, if I had a petition, it would be that you were happily married to some nice prince," Lady Kaye confided.

"Imagine that," Princess Mariposa said.

"Now. Seriously, you've turned down any number of suitable young men. Don't you want to be crowned Queen?"

Princess Mariposa rolled up the letter. Her father, the late King, had left a will that stated that the Princess could not be crowned Queen until she married.

"What man writes a letter proposing to a woman he's never met?" she asked.

"You won't always be young, you know," Lady Kaye continued. "Your dear, dear parents have been gone a long time now. Eliora needs a queen on the throne. You owe it to your people, if not to yourself."

"I'm not marrying some stranger," Princess Mariposa said.

"No, you shouldn't. I merely meant you might meet this King and see what he is like," Lady Kaye replied. "I have heard good reports of him."

Princess Mariposa waved Marci forward, and the Wardrobe Mistress proceeded to help her into the dress. I stood, hands clasped behind my back, watching the

Princess's transformation. The pointed waist made hers seem even smaller, and the dark emerald color suited her sea-blue eyes. She was so beautiful.

"Maybe," the Princess said doubtfully while Marci buttoned up the back. "But if he's anything like his letter, he's already in love with himself."

The Baroness winked at me. "Of course, my dear, there is always that very nice Prince Sterling. It's much too late in the year for him to hazard the trip back over the mountains to Tamzin. Perhaps you could arrange for his stay to become permanent?"

Princess Mariposa blushed a deep pink.

"My dear Mariposa," Lady Kaye said, inclining her head, "I'm only thinking of your best interests."

"Of course," the Princess agreed.

"But those interests do include one's subjects and the future of one's kingdom," Lady Kaye added.

Princess Mariposa sighed. I had the feeling that on the inside she rolled her eyes.

"It's her kingdom," I told the Baroness, unable to resist saying so.

Marci glared at me.

"Indeed," Lady Kaye said, caressing the knob of her cane. "And to what do we owe the pleasure of your company, Darling?"

"Lindy injured her arm, and Darling stepped right up to iron the Princess's court dress," Marci told her.

That wasn't *exactly* the way it happened, but Princess Mariposa beamed at me.

"Oh, my dear," she exclaimed, "you saved me from having to wear that dreadful black dress today!"

"A terrible fate indeed," the Baroness replied.

I ignored that. "You look beautiful in all your dresses," I told the Princess.

"Yes, she does," Lady Kaye said, rising. "Perhaps you should order some new clothes, Your Majesty. I hear Prince Sterling is partial to royal blue."

"I like him," I said. "And royal blue."

"Not you, too," Princess Mariposa said, wagging a finger at me. "Run along."

7

When the Princess's handkerchiefs, towels, and sheets were ironed, folded, and tucked neatly into the waiting laundry baskets, I dusted my hands off in satisfaction. The scent of lavender and fresh-pressed cotton hung in the air. Lindy insisted on personally putting things away in the Princess's drawers and cupboards. My work was done.

A quick glance around the wardrobe hall assured me that I was alone.

I fetched Lyric from the dressing room and hustled into the closet. A quick change and I'd be off to make friends with the Head Librarian. Outside the windows, an icy-blue winter sky gleamed. The sunlight shimmered through the stained-glass canary in the center of the window. I paused to look out over the frost-glazed lawns below.

Lyric chirped at me, swinging on his little gold perch.

"Do you need a quick breath of fresh air?" I offered, turning the crank on the side window.

I leaned out, breathing in. My fingertips burned on the icy sill. I closed my eyes and pressed a palm to the castle wall. Magic coursed through the castle, every stone and timber, every wall and spire—a rich, bubbling well of sensation akin to music, color, and joy, all tangled together.

"Hello," I whispered, and felt all the creatures echoing my greeting. They were stone and metal, plaster and resin, birds and animals from great to small, seemingly carved and added as decorations inside the castle and out. But they were actually real, alive and waiting, bound by the magic. A hummingbird far away in a drawing room tickled my mind.

I laughed and the castle laughed with me.

Then I sensed the dragons. Chained to the tallest spire, they brooded. I felt their talons sink into me and yank—hard. I pulled against them, struggling to get loose. The bitter cold of their hatred wrapped itself around my mind, *squeezing*.

And then they spoke to me.

We will break these collars. We will wreak vengeance on you!

"Me!" I squeaked. "Why me?"

But the dragons didn't answer. Instead, they flicked me away like some bug they couldn't waste time squishing.

I stumbled forward, gasping. My heart clanged against my rib cage as if it meant to abandon me to face the dragons on my own. I pressed a hand to my chest to prevent that from happening.

I grimaced; no dragon would get loose as long as I, Darling Fortune, was on guard. Break their collars, indeed! I doubted that was possible—as long as the magic coursed through the castle. Until someone wore the cuffs from the King's regalia and said the magic word, *Sarvinder,* to let them loose, the dragons would remain stuck where they were. I cranked the window closed. The dragons weren't going anywhere this afternoon.

"I need to take a little stroll," I said.

The dresses quivered. A bronze sleeve waved at me. I went over to Forty-Nine and lifted it off the hanger. Forty-Nine shone like burnished metal, dripping jet-black stones and sporting black lace trim. It consisted of a fitted dress with a short fitted jacket worn over it, quite unlike the other dresses. It had a serious air about it, seeming to blink owlishly at me. The perfect dress to wear to a library.

I shimmied into it. A fresh-faced young woman stared at me from the mirror. She wore the uniform of a Laundress. I recognized her; her name was Nina.

"No," I said. "This won't work. I'm not going to the under-cellar. I'm going to the King's library."

The dresses bristled as if the ruffles, flounces, and ribbons had developed sharp edges. Forty-Nine stiffened. I felt a twinge of conscience. I hadn't found out what Thirty-Seven wanted yet.

"Did you want to show me something?" I asked the dresses.

Forty-Nine bounced around my hips.

"It's downstairs in the under-cellar, isn't it?"

Lyric chirped. The dresses waited expectantly.

Laundresses did travel around the castle, picking up dirty laundry and delivering clean clothes. But they kept to the back stairs and side corridors. The library would have to wait.

"All right," I said, smothering a sigh, "let's go to the under-cellar."

The dresses hummed with approval. So I jogged down to the under-cellar, looking purposeful. It helped to act confident when I wore one of the dresses; no one questioned people who looked like they knew what they were doing.

When I reached the cellar stairs, Forty-Nine trembled. The jet-black stones dangling from the bodice tinkled as they collided with each other.

"What's wrong?" I whispered. "Are you scared?"

Light from the corridor above sifted down the stairs,

brushing the steps before filtering into the cellar. Shelves and bins full of boxes, crates, and sacks of food waited in the cool dimness. Silence rang through the cellar. Only the Kitchen Maids and the Footmen went in there. No one and nothing else, not even a mouse or a spider, disturbed its stillness.

"It's not dark in the under-cellar," I told the dress. "Let's go visit some Laundresses."

Forty-Nine jiggled in agreement, and I raced down the rest of the stairs, past the cellar to the under-cellar.

A steamy warmth greeted me. Two worlds existed in the under-cellar: the laundry and the scrubbing station. Clothes, bedding, and linens were washed in the laundry. Pots, pans, utensils, and dishes were washed in the scrubbing station. Great hearths lined both sides. It took an ocean of hot water to do all that washing and scrubbing. I inhaled the under-cellar's scent: soot, smoke, vinegar, and lavender. An odd bouquet indeed.

A rush of memories assailed me: months spent down here with Gillian. I scrubbed, she dried. I glanced around for her, but the scrub side was empty. On the laundry side, a knot of Laundresses stood over a basket of clean clothes.

They wore the sleeves of their brown dresses rolled up to their elbows, displaying their well-muscled arms. Laundresses scrubbed clothes over laundry boards, wielded heavy wooden paddles to dip clothes in boiling rinse water, and toted heavy loads up and down stairs all over the castle. They were strong. And not a little feisty.

A Laundress named Beatrice kicked the basket. Her damp tan apron lapped wetly against her front.

"I could swear it was right here!" Beatrice exclaimed.

"Are you sure?" Ursula asked, digging through the basket. "I don't see it."

"Well," Beatrice said, "I know it was here before we had our tea!"

"Lady Marguerite will be so mad!" Rayna offered, as if that helped.

"What's she want with a riding skirt in this weather?" Ursula asked.

"She's crazy, obviously. Thinks her horse gets lonely without her." Beatrice rolled her eyes. "She asked me to wash it special. Wants it right back. Like I've got nothing else to do."

"Nina," Rayna said, spying me, "have you seen Lady Marguerite's riding skirt?"

"No," I said, secretly relieved. No wonder Mrs. Pepperwhistle had believed me the other night. Lady Marguerite *did* have a horse.

"Check your station," Ursula suggested. "Maybe someone moved it."

"Sure," I said, going over to the area where Nina worked.

Forty-Nine jostled me along, and I tugged on its skirt.

If this was what the dress wanted me to see, I would—it didn't have to hurry me. Nina's niche gleamed, as if she spent more time scrubbing it than the clothes. Usually everything was in order, but today bars of soap, brushes, and laundry were strewn about.

"Do you see it?" I whispered to Forty-Nine, turning things over, making a bigger mess.

The dress pinched my waist.

"Not here," I called to the Laundresses.

A canvas flap across an opening in the brick wall flipped aside. Behind it was an alcove that the Head Laundress used as an office. Selma was the only one allowed to touch the Princess's clothes. She washed some garments, but the more fragile and costly dresses were brushed and sponged.

"Finish up," Selma said, bouncing out, a ball of pent-up energy.

"Lady Marguerite's riding skirt walked off all by itself," Beatrice said, snapping her fingers. "Like that."

"Have you searched all the stations?" Selma asked.

The Laundresses looked at one another.

"I checked mine," I said, angling for the stair.

Selma barked out orders. "You three look out here. Nina, go check the drying room."

"But I took it down and folded it," Beatrice protested.

"That skirt has to be somewhere," Selma said. "Look everywhere. We don't go losing folks' clothes."

I headed for the drying room. Forty-Nine sidled up my legs as I walked. I pushed it back down.

"You wanted to come here," I reminded the dress.

The drying room was all that remained of the original castle before it burned to the ground. To reach it, you had to walk down a hall that sloped upward. Along its jagged stone walls, you could still see scorch marks. Once upon a time it had been a dungeon.

It was a huge, echoing space, lit by windows high up that peeked out to wink at the sun. Long iron hooks that were used to open the windows dangled from pegs underneath. Mounted on poles, row after row of clotheslines stretched across the room, lined with wet clothes. In good weather, the windows were opened so that fresh air dried the clothes. In the winter, the clothes hung, sodden and drippy. Pools collected on the floor, making it slippery. The air steamed around me. Fires burned in hearths at the back wall, supposedly hastening the drying. In reality, clothes took forever to dry at this time of year. If Lady Marguerite's skirt was in here, she wouldn't be riding anytime soon.

Forty-Nine fidgeted as I walked around, careful of puddles. Every possible variety of clothing swung sagging from wooden pegs used to clamp them to the clothesline. I leaned closer to squint at a skirt-shaped object. Forty-Nine stiffened like a scrubbing board.

"I won't let you get wet," I told it.

A fat drop of water splatted at my feet. Forty-Nine twisted backward.

"Do you think it's in here?" I asked the dress.

Forty-Nine tugged at me to leave. I circled, taking one last look. No sign of a riding skirt. I hurried back down the hall.

The Laundresses and Selma were digging through a row of baskets.

"This doesn't belong in here!" Ursula announced, pulling out a pair of long johns.

"It's not in there," I said, ready to dash for the stair.

"Someone's gone and mixed everything around," Rayna whined.

"Mark my word, I'll find out who. And then there'll be trouble." Selma rubbed her chin with a red hand. A gleam lit her eyes.

"What'll I tell Lady Marguerite?" Beatrice asked.

"Nothing. We'll search till we find it," Selma said. "Nina, go call the others in the kitchens. This is an emergency."

8

"I hope you're happy," I told Forty-Nine as I jogged back up the stairs.

Rounding up the Laundresses and picking through a castle-load of clean clothes had eaten away a lot of time. Shadows lined the walls and hounded at my heels. No telling if the Princess was dressing for dinner now. Or if Lindy had returned to put away the clothes. Or where Marci might be. I had to get back into that closet super quick.

As I raced down a corridor, Francesca rounded the corner. I froze, clutching Forty-Nine like a life preserver.

Francesca stopped short. Her black braids swung ominously. Her gray eyes opened wide, as if she couldn't believe what she was seeing.

"What are you doing here?" she demanded.

"Um," I said, my brain as frozen over as the lawn.

"The clean laundry was delivered early this morning, and the soiled laundry was taken away at the same time. So," she said, "what are *you* doing here?"

Nina, whom Francesca thought she was talking to, was going to be in big trouble. I had to get her—and me—out of this fast.

I tossed my head to show her I was not scared. "I am not here for soiled clothes," I said as if this was obvious. "I'm running an errand."

"What errand?"

"A message for the Wardrobe Mistress," I said.

Francesca chewed that over for a minute. "Let me see it," she said.

A bead of sweat broke out on my forehead. Then I remembered that a lot of the Laundresses couldn't read or write. I threw my hand over my heart.

"Are you mocking me?" I wailed. "You mean, mean girl! I'll tell the Head Laundress, I will. See if I don't!"

Francesca rolled her eyes. "All right, go deliver your message."

Sobbing theatrically, I hurried off with Francesca stuck to my side. I couldn't shake her. If I turned the wrong way, she'd surely stop me. So I headed straight to the wardrobe hall.

Marci was seated at the desk, writing in one of the

white leather-covered books. She glanced up as I walked in with Francesca on my heels.

"Yes?" she asked.

"I have a message for you," I replied.

"Oh." She arched an eyebrow.

I could feel Francesca breathing down my neck.

"A personal message," I added, hoping Francesca would take the hint.

"I found her wandering around the hall," Francesca said, as if reporting a serious crime.

"I missed my way," I said quickly. "And I was not wandering. I was coming straight here."

A little too quickly. A suspicious gleam lit Marci's eyes.

"Thank you for directing her, Francesca. I won't keep you." Marci smiled, a wolfish, gold-capped-tooth smile that never failed to instill fear in Under-scrubbers.

Francesca wavered. But Marci outranked her, so she turned on her heel and stalked out.

I sagged against the desk.

"Let's hear this message, girlie," Marci said.

"Um, well, the Head Laundress said to tell you that she—"

"The Head Laundress, eh?" Marci folded her hands over her stomach. "Go on. Oh, I should mention that I intend to verify your source."

"Uh ...," I said.

"I thought so," Marci purred. "Darling, get in that closet and take off that dress before I send you downstairs to work for Selma for the rest of your days."

Relieved, I nodded and hurried into the closet.

"I didn't get to the library," I mumbled under my breath.

Forty-Nine sagged in my hands as I took it off and deposited it on its hanger.

"But Marci didn't squeal on me either. *That* was good," I said, giving Forty-Nine a little pat to show it that there were no hard feelings before going back out.

Only to find Francesca once again standing at Marci's desk. She had her back to me. I slid over to the pressing room door and gripped the knob.

"She just left," Marci told her.

"I didn't see her in the hall," Francesca said.

Marci shrugged. "Well, no one's here now. Are they, Darling?"

"Nope," I said, releasing the knob and dusting off my hands. "All finished."

"Excellent," Marci said.

Francesca eyed me as if she knew something was wrong but couldn't put her finger on it. "You know the Laundresses. What was her name?"

"Whose name?"

"The girl who was here."

I shrugged. "She didn't come in the pressing room."

"You've been in there the whole time?" she demanded.

"Some of us have been working," I said.

"And some of us ought to be," Marci added.

Francesca turned a bright shade of scarlet. It went well with her dark hair. She glowered at me as if somehow her confusion was my fault, and then she left.

I relaxed, ready to waltz downstairs and look for Gillian. I still owed her a story. Before I could go, a steely-cold voice stopped me.

"Those dresses aren't playthings," Marci said.

"I know."

"Do you? If you get caught," Marci said, "not even I will be able to save you."

"I won't get caught," I said.

Marci arched an eyebrow. "This isn't a game. Her Majesty likes you—*trusts* you—but don't think that can't change. Betray her confidence and you might not get it back."

9

Francesca dogged my steps after that, turning up where she wasn't expected—or wanted. I stumbled over her coming out of the washroom. She popped up outside the pressing room. If I visited the greenhouses to see Jane and the other Pickers, she lingered outside, stamping her feet in the cold. At dinner, she loitered at a nearby table.

Didn't that girl have anything else to do?

I didn't dare go near the closet. Whenever Lindy left the room, I heard the dresses clanging their hangers. I'd been to the under-cellar, like they wanted. I got the message: someone had poked around in the Laundresses' stations. I wasn't sure what they expected me to do about it, other than to keep an eye out for mischief. And it wasn't as if I could be down there all the time. I had work to do.

And a Librarian to talk to, just as soon as I could figure out how.

But Marci was right. Being caught wearing one of Queen Candace's dresses could get me thrown out of the castle. I worked, tiptoeing around Lindy, who wore her bandaged arm like a medal earned in battle. She hadn't liked it that I'd ironed the Princess's dress. That was *her* job, she reminded me. I knew better than to argue. I did my work and then escaped to the safety of the under-cellar.

It was the one place where Francesca had no excuse to follow me.

The first time I showed up, Selma interrogated me. Had I been down there recently? Touched anything I shouldn't? Seen anyone around who shouldn't be?

"No, ma'am," I assured her, crossing my heart.

She cuffed me playfully on the head. "Go bother some-one else, then," she told me.

I waltzed off to spend my free time telling Gillian stories.

Every evening, Roger nagged me. He was almost as bad as the dresses.

"We should go ghosting," he insisted.

Ghosting. Whatever it was, it sounded spooky.

"What's ghosting?" I said.

"That's when you go sneaking around looking for stuff you can't see," he said.

"Why?" I asked.

"Because," he said, "there's safety in numbers."

That didn't answer my question.

I'd decided that whatever I saw in the corridor that evening was only my imagination. There were no such things as ghosts. Therefore, there weren't any in the castle. I wasn't sneaking around the castle in the dark without a good reason.

And so far Roger hadn't supplied one.

But one evening, his pestering gave me an idea. Francesca was supposed to be with her mother in the Upperservants' lounge. Here was my chance to use a dress. But just in case Francesca wasn't where she was supposed to be, I needed a lookout. And I knew the Stable Boy for the job.

"I'm going to the library," I told him, dragging him into the closet, "and I need you to keep me safe."

"Safe from what?" he asked, glancing at the dresses.

"Ghosts," I said.

Roger stood a little straighter. "You think there might be ghosts in the library?" he asked, yanking off his cap.

The dresses clanged their hangers together. Roger wrung his cap in his hands.

"Nobody, but nobody, goes anywhere near there," I said, dropping my voice.

He nodded, all ears.

"Don't you suppose that's because something spooky lurks around that part of the castle?" I asked.

Roger's eyelid twitched.

I let that soak in a moment, and then I added, "You can go ghosting outside the library while I hunt inside."

He nodded slowly. "You'd be in calling distance if you got in trouble."

I ground my teeth together. *He'd* be in calling distance if *he* got in trouble. *I'd* be the one with the disguise, able to swoop in to save *him*. But I nodded; he'd been ready to walk me upstairs that evening after we saw—whatever it was.

"Good plan, Darling," Roger added, brightening.

The dresses rustled in agreement. *They* were ready.

Seventy-Seven wiggled a silver ribbon at me. I picked up the lilac satin with its silvery white underskirt and held it out.

"We have a volunteer," I told Roger.

I unbuttoned it. Roger stepped back, giving me—and the dress—a wide berth. I slipped the dress on, and it whizzed around me, snuggling up tight. In the mirror, I saw the reflection of a girl a few years older than me, with long dark blond hair tied up in a velvet bow. She wore a purple velvet gown and batted her green eyes at me. She wasn't very big or very tall. She was like a miniature lady-in-waiting, all velvet and jewels, except for her slightly crooked smile. I liked her at once.

"Who is she?" Roger squinted at me.

"Somebody who can visit the library."

Roger squared his cap on his head and we sailed off. I'd done a lot of listening the past few days to whomever I could get talking, hoping to learn more about the Librarian. That Sweeper was right; he never left his library, and he was very choosy about whom he talked to. Evidently, Under-pressers were not his idea of interesting people to chat with.

Not that I'd actually set foot inside the library. Yet. But all that listening hadn't been a waste of time. Oh, no. I'd learned a few juicy morsels about my quarry. The Librarian's name was Master Varick. He had camped in the library for the last twenty years, favored lemon cookies, and imagined himself the keeper of great secrets. Nobody else thought he had any to keep, but maybe everyone was wrong.

I, Darling Fortune, Under-presser, had the biggest secret in the castle: the magic in the hundred dresses. Only Marci knew about that. And Roger. Despite what the others thought, the Librarian could be hoarding the deepest, darkest secrets imaginable.

At the very least, he could recommend a good book.

We hurried down to the second floor and coasted along the deserted corridor to the southwest corner. Roger nodded at me encouragingly and set off on his own. A pair of great carved doors guarded the King's library, with a snarling lion's-head doorknob standing sentinel on each. Gingerly, I turned one. The brass lion's teeth pricked my palm. I snatched my hand back as the great door opened, gliding silently away from me to reveal a patch of inlaid floor.

A breath flowed out to me, a curious mixture of paper, leather, and lemon oil, as if the library exhaled at my approach. Ridiculous—the library certainly hadn't been holding its breath! But when I stepped across the threshold, every hair on my body rose; every nerve tingled. Seventy-Seven scrunched against me. I froze. Rows and rows and tiers and tiers of books soared to the carved ceiling above. Thousands of books. More than one person could open, let alone read, in a lifetime. The air around me crackled with excitement.

Those books ached to be read, just as the dresses yearned to be worn.

I glanced back, anxious to spot Roger in the corridor, but he was out of sight. I turned into the library. I had a dress and a mission. I couldn't falter now.

Shafts of light from lamps set here and there on tables fell on the floor's inlaid squares, guiding my footsteps.

I gravitated to the nearest shelf. Cracked leather covers squinted at me in the dim light, the dyed leather faded and worn. Tracings of gilded titles, rubbed thin by many fingers, glinted at me. My hand lifted of its own accord and sought a book, my fingers grazing the edges of the covers until they curled around one and snatched it off the shelf.

The book fell open in my hand. And magic poured out of it into my skin. The letters blurred on the page as the magic jumped and pulsed. The printed words danced. The music sang out.

I gasped; the books were as full of magic as the dresses, if not more so. Startled, I snapped the book shut and shoved it back on the shelf. The books hummed at me. I took a step backward. The humming sharpened as if they were demanding I read them.

But I hadn't come for that; I'd come to find things out from the Librarian.

"You there! What are you doing?" an indignant voice called.

I whirled around and found a stooped, thin man stepping out from behind a bookcase. A shock of white hair fell across his forehead, obscuring his sharp blue eyes. He wore a long formal coat that must have once been costly but now was covered all over in patches of every color. The effect was such that he blended in with the bookshelves.

"Well," he said, squinting at me, "what have you to say for yourself?"

My mouth fell open, but nothing came out. I hadn't actually planned what I'd say to the Librarian if I found him.

"Have you come for a book?" he prompted. "A volume of poetry, perhaps?"

I stood frozen and mute; all my cleverness had deserted me.

"Well?" he demanded.

"I've been wondering about Magnificent Wray," I blurted out.

The Librarian sucked on his teeth. "Magnificent Wray?"

I nodded. "He has an interesting tombstone."

He clasped his hands behind his back and rocked on his heels. "What would Lady Sara be doing mucking about with tombstones?"

What *would* Lady Sara be doing in the cemetery?

"Um . . ." I decided that the closer I stayed to the truth, the better. "Warden Graves showed it to me."

He frowned. "Nobody reads *those* books."

"What books?" I asked, fighting the urge to shake him.

"I have that collection of fairy tales. Had to replace the spine, but still, if you're careful . . . I could let you borrow that."

I patted my skirt. Seventy-Seven quivered under my fingertips.

"Thank you, but I'd like a book on Magnificent Wray, please."

He harrumphed, turning back to the recesses of the library. I tripped after him, anxious not to lose him in the dimness. He walked to a dark corner where a series of bookcases with smoke-tinted glass doors stood like indignant old ladies clutching their books to their chests. I squinted through the gray glass, unable to read any titles on the books' spines.

The Librarian dug in his pockets, produced a small brass key, and unlocked a case. I held my breath as the glass door opened and the books were revealed. Cracked, faded, and worn from use, the battered row of ancient books expelled a rich perfume of roses. Dark, dried petals were scattered everywhere—on the shelves and littering the tops of the books.

The Librarian ran his bony finger along the row until he touched a dark cherry-red spine. He inched the book out, carefully dusting the petals aside. He held the book, caressing its cover, which was blackened in spots by the oil from numerous fingertips.

My fingers itched. An overpowering urge to grab the book out of his hands possessed me. I gritted my teeth and hung on to Seventy-Seven.

The Librarian held the volume out to me; the gold-inscribed title glinted in the lamplight: *Magnificent Reflections.*

"This book comes from the King's private collection. It's priceless." He coughed. "Take special care of it and return it promptly. Please," he added, as if he realized he was speaking to a member of the Princess's court.

"I promise I will, Master Varick," I replied, closing my hands around the book, shivering with the thrill of the magic that buzzed under my skin.

10

I walked out of the library, hugging the book to my heart. Finally I would know who the Wrays were and what made them special. I opened the cover.

The Thoughts and Ideas of Magnificent Wray, the page read.

Magic bubbled up through me, making my hair dance and my nerves sing. I couldn't *wait* to read this book! I ran my finger down the book's gilded edges. The pages parted and fell open. Spidery lines flowed across the paper, tracing the outline of the great cathedral in the city. Notes were scribbled in a cramped corner: measurements that meant nothing to me. I turned the page. More spidery outlines. I turned the book sideways. This drawing looked like the cathedral cut in half.

The next page held elaborate drawings of stained-glass windowpanes. Smears of colors ran down the side of the page. Each color had a number next to it, and those numbers also appeared inside the window. I flipped faster: drawings of beetles, a little girl, and a house; mathematical equations; and lists—umber, indigo, linseed oil, chalk. Ingredients?

And then faded handwriting, a tangle of loops and whorls, as if the words had danced out of Magnificent Wray's pen and onto the paper. *Vision compels action. What is illuminated is truly seen.* None of it made sense, but the words themselves tingled with magic.

I shuffled past several pages until a single sentence caught my eye: *Light shines.*

I felt a throb under my breastbone. Somehow, some way, these words mattered. I put a fingertip on the handwriting. The magic there vibrated as if the pen had just left the page. It was like the magic coursing through the castle, but different. Like musical notes. The pitch was lower. Deeper. Like the sound of a rock plunked into a pond.

I could almost see ripples in the air. The magic rang like a bell striking midnight. My lungs tightened. My heart hammered. A bead of sweat trickled down my face. I slammed the book shut.

This wasn't any ordinary book. It held thoughts and

ideas. And not any old stuff ... extraordinary thoughts. Magical ideas. This book couldn't be gulped down like a glass of milk; it needed to be sipped slowly, like hot chocolate. I had to sit down and study these pages one by one.

But I couldn't, because Roger the Freckled Ghost-hunter was on his hands and knees, crawling along the baseboard. Clutching the book, I tiptoed down the hall and snuck up behind him.

"What are you doing?" I asked. "Looking for *tiny* ghosts?"

Roger jumped; his cap slid over one eye. He snatched it off and rocked back on his heels, glowering.

"Course not. I felt a draft."

I grinned. "What do drafts have to do with ghosts?"

He shook his head. "You don't know much about ghosts."

I put a hand on my hip. "And you do?"

He nodded. "Lots of talk out in the stables."

"Don't tell me, let me guess. Ghosts like horses."

He shot to his feet, leaning toward me so that his nose was only inches away from mine. "You think you know so much, Darling. But for all you know, every one of those dresses is haunted."

I swallowed. Hard. That was ridiculous.

"So what is the talk in the stables?" I asked.

"You know the saying *as cold as the grave*?" Roger asked.

"Yeah?" I trembled involuntarily.

"They say that 'cause the dead are cold. A ghost chills the air wherever it goes. So some drafts are drafts, but some are ghost trails. See?"

I nodded. It made a weird sort of sense.

"I felt a draft," he said, his breath tickling my cheek. "I followed it until it disappeared."

His face glowed with the thrill of his hunt. He was almost handsome.

"Right into the wall," he said, eyes shining.

I took a step back. The book tingled beneath my fingertips. Then I felt a sliver of cold air graze my cheek and set me shivering.

"I should get back," I said. "We'll have to do more ghosting another night."

"Yeah." He nodded. "We will."

We walked to the main staircase and went our separate ways. It was only about the middle of the evening, but shadows filled the corridors. Dark shapes danced against the windows. I heard a faint tapping. I stopped, clutching my precious book like a shield.

All this talk of ghosts was making me nervous. I marched to the window to peer outside. Snowflakes flitted past the glass.

I exhaled.

Of course I'd felt cold. It wasn't proof of ghosts; it was winter!

I raced back to the closet and put Seventy-Seven away. Then I stood caressing my book and looking about for a hiding place for it. I couldn't leave it lying just anywhere, and I certainly couldn't carry it around with me. There was no place in the closet to put it.

I walked out into the wardrobe hall, thinking. Marci would be furious if she found the book in her drawers. The pressing room? Lindy with a bandaged burn was crabbier than usual. I didn't want *her* to find it. I needed to put the book someplace where I could get hold of it when I had time to read it—

Where could I go to read a book I couldn't be seen having?

I chewed my lower lip. What a pickle!

It was then I heard muffled sobbing coming from under Marci's desk. If all the stories are correct, ghosts don't sob; they wail. I slipped the book onto the desktop and looked under it.

Dulcie huddled in the darkness like a little wet hen, her bedraggled braids working loose of their ribbons. Tears glistened on her cheeks. She had gathered up her apron to use as a handkerchief.

"Are you sick?"

She shook her head.

"Have they been picking on you again?" I asked.

"N-no," she blubbered.

"Then what's wrong?"

She gulped air and wiped at her eyes.

"You can tell me, Dulcie. I won't tell anyone. I'm good at keeping secrets."

"I miss my family," she whispered.

"Oh," I said, and plopped down on the floor beside her. "Tell me about them."

"We all used to live on our farm together, me and my two big brothers and two little brothers."

"That sounds like a nice family," I said, wishing I had one.

"I always took my younger brother to gather eggs."

"What's his name?" I asked.

"Cole; and then there's Andy, Charlie, and baby Phillip."

"I bet they all miss you."

"Really?"

"Sure. But I bet they're proud of you too. Not every girl is a Princess's Girl."

She thought that over and nodded.

"Are you going to be okay?" I asked, remembering my book.

"I'm okay." She wiped her nose with the back of her hand. I dug in my pocket and handed her a clean hand-kerchief.

"Thanks," she whispered.

"Don't forget to put that in the laundry," I said. Francesca kept a close count of items like stockings and handkerchiefs.

I stood up, walked around the desk, and reached back across to pick up my book so Dulcie couldn't see me grab it. Then I took it and hid it in the one place I could think of.

The wooden crate stamped ARTICHOKES.

11

The next morning, the rosy glow of dawn dappled the white eiderdown coverlets on the dormitory beds and turned the polished wood floor to a glossy cinnamon. I inhaled the lavender scent of the sheets as a tiny paw tapped me on the tip of my nose.

"Morning, Iago," I mumbled through a yawn. "Hope you don't mind sharing the box."

He twitched his whiskers and curled his tail. I wasn't sure what that meant, so I changed the subject. "Why do the dragons hate me so much?" I asked.

He eyed me as if this was a dumb question. Dragons hate everyone.

"Well, I know why, but why *me*?"

His tiny black eyes flashed. Then he vanished under my pillow and emerged with my aquamarine hair ribbon in his teeth. He shook it at me and dropped it onto my pillow.

I picked it up and curled it around my finger.

"Because they hate ribbons?"

Iago put a paw over his eyes.

I thought harder. The ribbon had been a gift from the Princess.

"Because of the Princess?"

He threw his paws wide and staggered back as if in amazement at my genius. I frowned. Sometimes he was a little overly dramatic.

"But she hasn't done anything to them," I argued.

And she hadn't. Sure, she owned the castle, but she hadn't built it or chained up the dragons. Did she even know they were real?

Iago crawled over my forehead and up on the post of my bed, where my locket hung. He lunged at it. Caught it in his paws and started it swinging. Then he looped back to my pillow and waited, ears tuned.

"My locket," I said, closing my fist around it. "Huh?"

Across the room, Francesca sat up and stretched. Iago vanished under the bed.

"Everybody up!" Francesca called, rubbing her eyes.

I fought the urge to groan. Trust Francesca to interrupt. I rolled out of bed, and so did the other Princess's Girls. I dressed, mulling the matter over in my mind.

What was Iago trying to say about the locket?

While I worked, I thought about the magic buried in the pages of Magnificent Wray's book. Which made me wonder: why was the magic in the castle walls, the dresses, and the library books, but not in the pots or draperies or furniture? Why was I the only one who was aware of it? Once I read the book, would I possess powerful secrets? Could I harness the magic? Make it do my bidding?

The thought made me shudder. Maybe I shouldn't read that book.

Maybe it was dangerous.

I shook that off; Master Varick wouldn't have let some lady of the court have a perilous book, would he? I didn't think so. He knew who she was.

He knew who she was.

How could I return the book once I'd read it? I couldn't wear Seventy-Seven again, and I'd never seen the same person twice in the mirror. I sighed so loudly that Lindy glared at me.

Finding answers was a complicated business. I'd just

have to read the book and think of some way to sneak it back into the library.

Which made me curious: could I put on a different dress and borrow another book?

Once Lindy had gone off to nurse her sore arm by drinking tea with the Head Cook, I sidled over to the closet and opened the door.

"What do you think you're up to?" Marci asked, appearing out of a closet with a shawl over her arm.

"Nothing," I said.

"You almost got into real trouble the other day," she began.

"But I didn't."

Marci arched an eyebrow, pinning me to the floor with her stare.

The dresses flapped disappointedly. I shut the closet door.

Marci held out the white shawl edged with tassels. "Her Highness said to send this down to Selma. And since you don't appear to have any useful work to do, you can take it for me."

"Yes, ma'am," I said, folding it over my arm.

I headed off to the under-cellar, arriving as the Scrubbers were finishing up for the afternoon. A stray bubble drifted my way. I caught it on the tip of my finger. It glistened with a thousand colors until it popped, vanishing into thin air. With a sigh, I walked across the hard floor, searching for Selma.

I spied a cluster of Under-dryers stacking the last of the pots.

Gillian dried her hands on the towel tied around her waist. Her dark curls had tightened in the steamy fog that hung in the air. The hem of her brown dress sagged with moisture, and her canvas apron had a streak across it.

She smiled when she saw me. "Come for a visit?"

"I have to deliver this to the Head Laundress. Have you seen her?"

"Halloo," Selma called from across the room, waving me over.

I walked to her and held out the shawl. "Marci sent it," I said.

Selma held it up, admiring it. "How lovely. Doesn't even look like it's been worn," she said. "That Princess heard about my missing shawl and offered me one of her own."

"Oh," I said, "really?"

Selma bobbed her head. "Oh yes, insisted. And here it is! Too nice to wear, of course. But lovely all the same."

Gillian ambled over, yanking off her apron.

"But it's too pretty *not* to wear!" Gillian exclaimed. "Try it on."

"Well, a quick try-on." Selma wrapped the shawl around

her shoulders. Her dark eyes sparkled as she clutched the shawl's ends together in her chapped hand, turning this way and that, showing off her prize. "Do I look like a regular queen?"

"You do!" Gillian and I agreed.

"Get along." Selma blushed. She took the shawl off and folded it carefully. A tear glistened on her cheek. "Such a kindness," she murmured. "My favorite color."

"White?" I'd never heard of it being anyone's favorite color before.

Selma nodded. "It's the same color as the one that went missing."

"Let's go." Gillian grabbed me.

Selma's head popped up. "Wait, Darling. I was a-wondering: what color of shawl does Lindy wear?"

She had the same gleam in her eye she'd had when Lady Marguerite's riding skirt went missing. It wasn't a look I liked to see.

"She wears a long black cloak. I've never seen her with a shawl."

"How'd you say she got burned?" The gleam in Selma's eye intensified.

I hadn't said.

"Um, one of her irons, I think," I said. At least, that's what I assumed had happened. Marci hadn't ever said.

Gillian bounced on her toes, eager to leave.

"It wasn't boiling water?"

"I don't think so," I replied. What did shawls and boiling water have to do with anything?

"You girls run along now," Selma said.

"Bye," Gillian said, and hauled me off to the stair. "I heard," she said as we climbed, "that you've seen a ghost."

Roger the Freckled Blabbermouth!

"I'm not saying it was a ghost. It might have been anything."

"Like what?"

"Like . . . well, like . . . ," I sputtered.

"Were you scared?" she asked.

"Maybe a little. For a minute, but it was a trick of the light or my imagination—"

"Ooh, it's all so exciting." Gillian twisted her hands together, eyes shining. "Whose ghost do you think it is?"

I shrugged.

"A brokenhearted lady, an abandoned child, or a *murder* victim," Gillian breathed, "from some horrible unsolved crime."

"Uh."

"Did it seem sad or angry or"—Gillian gulped—"evil?"

A shiver crept down my spine. My knees knocked together. I stopped right there.

"There aren't any ghosts," I said.

A frown creased her heart-shaped face. "Don't be silly. If there are dragons, there are ghosts!"

I had no argument to refute that. But the logic of it filled me with a gnawing unease. I wasn't afraid of dragons . . . well, not so long as they stayed put. But *ghosts*? My whole being twitched nervously at the thought.

What if I'd *really* seen a ghost? The specter took shape in my mind—and weight, pushing back my resistance. A tremor ran down my leg. Somewhere a phantom, secreted in some shadowed nook, waited to haunt the castle corridors once more. I pictured it growing denser and darker, eager to come out.

"The Princess took you to that cemetery to see your mother's grave," Gillian continued, oblivious to my discomfort.

I flinched.

She leaned closer. "Maybe it's your mother's ghost, and she's followed you home."

"No, the ghost showed up before then," I protested.

"Aha!" Gillian exclaimed. "So you *did* see a ghost!"

She trembled with excitement; now there was no chance that she'd stop until she had answers.

"May . . . be," I said.

Gillian squealed with delight.

"Hush," I said, dragging her up the stairs, away from any listening ears below.

"So who do you think it is?" she asked. "Maybe it's a long-ago queen. Or it could be a servant!"

We arrived at the upper-cellar landing and started up for the kitchens.

Who was this ghost?

"Some overeager Upper-duster who fell while trying to clean the crown molding?" I said, picturing the accident.

"Could be!"

Suppose the ghost *had* been a servant? Servants tidied things up—like misplaced ribbons.

"You've heard lots of stories," I began.

"Most of them from you," Gillian said with a laugh.

"Not all."

"No, not all," she agreed.

"So in all those stories, have you ever heard of a ghost who could pick stuff up and move it?"

She chewed on her lower lip. "I'm not sure. Moving objects around doesn't sound very ghostly. Usually, ghosts walk through walls or wail or scare people. Stuff like that."

"But what if they could?"

Her dark eyes twinkled. "Maybe I can go with you and Roger on your next ghost hunt and find out?"

"Um ..." My voice caught in my throat. Despite what I'd told Roger, I didn't plan to go looking anytime soon. "I—I'll think about it."

"Deal!" she said, grabbing my hand and shaking it.

12

Winter tightened its grip on the castle. Snow swirled around the towers, and icicles hung at the windows. Extra blankets appeared on the Girls' beds, and pairs of new slippers lined the dormitory. I wiggled my toes in their toasty warmth as I dressed in the morning. Even so, I scurried to get ready, eager to jump out of my nightclothes and into my dress before the sharp air nipped me.

Several Girls came down with nasty colds and were tucked back into bed. Which meant that someone was always in the dormitory, night and day, their wheezing and sneezing standing between me and the secrets of Magnificent Wray's book. But it also meant that Francesca was distracted, having to get the same amount of work done with fewer Girls. She had less time to spy on me.

"I'm back!" I sang as I waltzed into the closet with the birdcage.

The dresses vibrated with delight. Several reached out sleeves or ribbons, tempting me in their direction. I set the cage down on the table and pretended to think, a finger against my chin.

"What do you think, Lyric? Should I take one out for a walk?"

Lyric preened his feathers, as if to suggest his total indifference.

I ran a finger along the shoulders of the dresses, feeling the buzz of magic beneath my fingertip.

"Who'd like to go to the library?" I'd botched my first visit. I hadn't asked any questions. I still didn't know if Master Varick knew anything about the Wrays.

Twenty-Seven clanged its hanger against a bouncing Twenty-Eight.

"You?" I asked Twenty-Seven, picking it up.

The vivid pink dress, sparkling with crystals and gold embroidery, rippled around my forearm in a wave of flounces. I slid it on and it quivered into shape, squeezing my waist excitedly before settling down.

A woman with silver curls greeted me in the mirror. She wore a black dress with a plaid shawl pinned at the front with a ruby brooch. I'd seen her before around the castle. Her sparkling blue eyes hinted at a warm sense of humor.

"You'll be hard for Master Varick to say no to," I told the mirror.

Twenty-Seven fluttered its flounces in agreement.

I headed out the door and through the wardrobe room only to run into Princess Mariposa in the corridor.

"Marie!" she exclaimed. "What a pleasant surprise."

The Princess wore a silver-gray dress with charcoal trim and the same emerald pin she'd worn to the cemetery. The pin seemed too bright and cheery for the somber dress, but I'd noticed her wearing it a lot in recent days.

"Good afternoon, Your Highness," I said, hoping for a polite hello and a quick escape.

But the Princess had other ideas. She took me by the elbow.

"Oh, Marie, if you have a moment, I'd like to speak with you privately."

I squirmed in my borrowed dress. I'd always enjoyed spending time with the Princess, but hearing things meant for other people's ears made me uncomfortable. What could I say? What excuse would Marie make?

"Of course," I replied. Hopefully, she would want to tell Marie something unimportant, like Baron Somebody had bad breath.

Princess Mariposa led me into her private suite. She hurried to a door I knew all too well. As her hand turned the knob, a lump formed in my throat. She opened the door and waved me inside. The gallery gleamed a blinding white, from the floors to the walls to the white velvet curtains at the white-trimmed windows. And scattered over all that white sparkled a sea of butterflies in cases, mounted in white picture frames and set in white cabinets and curios.

"Well?" Princess Mariposa said. "Do you see?"

I gave an involuntary glance toward the ceiling. White butterflies had once hung from silver cords up there. They used to dance in the breeze of the open window. They were Princess Mariposa's private joy. But now an empty arc loomed overhead.

"They're gone," I said. The lump in my throat hardened into a rock.

"Marie, what do you think happened to them?" she asked.

Marie probably had no idea, but I did. I had let them loose. Not that I was about to tell the Princess.

I shook my head.

"There was that day," Princess Mariposa said, "when the whole courtyard was filled with butterflies."

I'd never forget *that* day in a million years. That was when she'd almost married that imposter, Dudley. I'd deliberately let the stone gryphon loose to stop the wedding— right after I'd accidentally set the butterflies free.

"Maybe something caused them to get loose," I offered, hoping that she'd think some*thing* wasn't some*one*.

She nodded slowly. "Maybe. Maybe they were trying to warn me."

The rock in my throat dropped to the pit of my stomach.

"I thought it was true love," she whispered. "How could I have been so wrong?"

Her eyes filled with the look she'd had the day she'd taken me to the Royal Cemetery—that longing for something she couldn't find.

"He fooled everyone," I said. *Everyone but me.*

A frown creased her forehead. "He didn't fool my Under-presser."

The rock grew to a boulder.

The Princess's lip trembled; she wanted an answer.

"Well," I said, trying to sound as grown up as possible, "nobody notices servants—or children. Maybe she overheard someone."

"Perhaps, but shouldn't I have known?" she demanded. "Or realized that my Wardrobe Mistress, Cherice, was in league with him the whole time?"

I wiped my sweaty palm on Twenty-Seven, which bunched under my hand in protest. I'd never liked Dudley, the fake Prince Baltazar. Not for a minute. Even before I'd overheard him plotting with Cherice—only I hadn't known it was her. She'd been so kind to me that I'd never suspected her.

I'd been deceived just like the Princess.

"She came highly recommended. Can you imagine?" Princess Mariposa continued.

"She's gone now, and so is that imposter," I said quickly. "It might be better to forget about it."

The Princess eyed me as if that wasn't what she had expected Marie to say.

Twenty-Seven tensed as though it meant to run off without me. And I was tempted to escape myself. I thought longingly of all those magic-filled books waiting in the library for someone to open them. And a Librarian full of answers, the very thing I longed for and couldn't find. If I was Darling Dimple Wray Fortune, then who did that make me?

Princess Mariposa ran her hand over a butterfly-filled cabinet with a sigh.

My heart throbbed. First and foremost, I was the Princess's Under-presser! I loved her and the castle and the Under-servants and—I realized what the Princess wanted. The very thing she'd thought she'd found but hadn't.

"I know you'll find true love, Your Highness," I said.

"Thank you, Marie," she said after a long silence. "But I thought I was sure then; how can I be certain now? How can I ever trust myself again?"

She toyed with her pin.

I remembered the evening when the rare butterfly had flown into the dressing room. Princess Mariposa had been sure its appearance was a sign. The next morning she was engaged to the fake Prince Baltazar. She hadn't been sure before that.

"Maybe something made you think he was the right one?"

She laughed bitterly. "You mean like the moonlight?"

I shrugged helplessly. "A sign, perhaps?"

She rolled her pin between her fingers, a serious look lighting her eyes. "There was something that happened one night that made me feel . . . sure."

"What?" I asked, feeling like a phony.

"A butterfly. A very rare one. I thought it was a sign."

"If you were sure," I asked cautiously, "then why did you need a sign?"

Her eyes widened. "I never thought of that!"

"Maybe you weren't so sure."

Her forehead creased in thought. Twenty-Seven tugged at my knees, urging me to go. I wished I could, but I had no idea how to leave without offending Her Highness.

"You are always such a comfort," the Princess said at long last. "This gives me a great deal to think about."

"I'm glad I could help," I said.

Princess Mariposa sighed. "I apologize, Marie, for bothering you with all this. Allow me to offer you tea."

"How sweet of you," I said. Twenty-Seven sagged against me; I gave it a reassuring pat.

Princess Mariposa swept me off to a beautifully decorated room in the main wing. There I sat, sipping tea and nibbling on cake, while she told me about the petitions she'd received from her subjects.

I eyed the door, anxious lest the real Marie appear. Another day I'd have been thrilled to take tea with the Princess, but Twenty-Seven simmered around me, a constant reminder that time was passing and my chance to get into the library was dwindling with it.

"And what do you suppose the Baroness has suggested?" she asked.

"What?" I asked, balancing my dainty china cup on my knee.

"New clothes! What do you think, Marie? Should I order some?"

"Yes," I said. "A new court dress would be nice."

Princess Mariposa pinked with delight. "Oh, what color?"

"Royal blue?" I suggested just as a Footman popped through the door.

"His Highness, Prince Sterling!" the Footman announced.

Prince Sterling wore a beautiful royal-blue coat with silver buttons and held a book in one hand. I felt my face grow warm. I hoped he hadn't overheard my suggestion.

"I hope I'm not disturbing you," Prince Sterling said, flashing a warm smile.

"Not at all," I said, forgetting myself.

Princess Mariposa laughed. "I've been boring Marie with all my woes. Please join us."

Prince Sterling sat down next to the Princess.

"I thought you'd enjoy this," he said, holding out the book: *Butterflies of the Indigo Islands*.

She took it reverently.

"Oh," she said, opening it. Gorgeous illustrations of butterflies flitted across the paper. "Thank you."

"They're beautiful," the Prince said, leaning over to turn the page. "And I thought you'd rather have pictures than—"

"Than a real butterfly pinned down for display," she finished with a sparkle in her eyes.

"Yes," he said with a grin.

She turned another page, and we spent the rest of the afternoon admiring her new book.

13

The next day Lindy was her old self, buzzing around the pressing room, loading me down with linens that had to be ironed now—or else. Towels that didn't even look wrinkled. It was as if she was making up for her lost time. Or rather I was making up for it. She flipped her long straight hair over her shoulder and plucked a towel out from under my iron.

"Can't you move any faster?" Lindy asked. "Time's a-wastin', girl."

It sure was. I didn't have a spare moment to sneak a peek at that book or nab a dress or chat with Gillian. I ironed so many miles of fabric that my arms ached and my back hurt. When I hauled myself out of bed the next morning, I moved like an ancient Picker with a bad knee.

"Get going, Girls," Francesca boomed, all bright and chipper.

What did she have to be in such a good mood about? My hair snarled in my brush. My shoestring broke. And my breakfast roll was filled with apricot jam. I *hate* apricots. I chewed the sour filling while my crate stamped ARTICHOKES waited under my bed skirt, bursting with information I didn't have.

Information I *ought* to have!

A fiery determination burned away my gloom. I ate slowly as, one by one, the Girls hurried off to work. When the last had left, I knelt down by my bed and pulled out my box. Whisking the lid aside, I grabbed the book.

Magic sizzled in my fingertips, causing me to juggle the book between my hands. The crimson cover slapped open. A torn page waved at me. The top half was missing, but writing marched across the bottom:

> . . . *my great service accomplished.*
>
> *"Build my castle anew," His Highness had said.*
>
> *So I bade the dragons build to my design. But more than building was required; a structure more than stones, a mighty edifice of magic was urgently demanded.*
>
> *I drew out of past Wrays that which had made them special, mighty, and powerful. My reach was such that only the generations closest to me could be tapped. So*

I extracted wisdom, courage, joy, and tenacity: these I funneled into the very stones of the castle. Then I set the starburst seal on my efforts. On the day the stars were born, the light shone. And now its very emblem marked my work, holding it fast. The castle and the kingdom guarded! The dragons subdued! Oh, lasting peace!

Safety!

I was content then to set down my pen, to lay aside my charge, and to withdraw. For what greater gift might a subject give his sovereign?

—M

The words were written in scarlet ink and seared into the page. Beneath them a starburst, crudely but decisively drawn, glimmered. Magic bubbled in its lines. . . . My finger drifted toward it.

The words *drew out of past Wrays* flashed at me. My finger halted an inch above the paper. I remembered the marvelous tombs of the Wrays dwindling into small stones in the Royal Cemetery. Warden Graves had been wrong. Those Wrays hadn't made bad choices. They'd been plundered by Magnificent himself! Their wisdom, courage, joy, and tenacity had been yanked free and poured into the castle.

And sealed by the starburst.

I snatched my finger back and slammed the book

shut. If *I* was a Wray, then what did this say about me? Was I lacking wisdom or joy or courage or tenacity? A cold sweat broke out on my forehead. I dumped the book in my box as if my hands might catch fire and slammed on the lid. Then, using my foot, I shoved my crate back under the bed.

My ribbon dangled over my eyebrow. I pulled it free, slicked back my hair, and retied it. Bright morning shone through the windows. How much time had passed while I'd stared at those words? I had to get to work.

As I jogged down the castle corridors, a strange sensation overtook me. The castle grew around me. It loomed larger and larger. And I shrank in comparison. Small. Insignificant. As tiny as a mouse. A weak, insignificant splat of nothing. I stumbled over a carpet and grabbed the wall to keep from falling.

Magic bubbled under the stones, caressing my hand. *The last Wray,* it whispered to me.

The truth struck me like a blinding light: no wonder the dragons hated me! I was a Wray! A Wray with a starburst-sealed locket! An empty one, to be sure, but a magic-kissed one all the same. Magnificent hadn't used himself to create the magic. He'd used the people who'd come before him—the dead Wrays. *Only the generations closest to me could be tapped,* he'd written. And in doing so he'd changed their individual destinies, but not his own.

No wonder the once-mighty Wrays had dwindled down to my mother the Under-chopper.

Magnificent had not stolen only from those long-ago Wrays; he *had* stolen something from me: my future prospects and my place. Where would I be now if he hadn't done it?

A great lady? A countess? A princess married to a foreign prince?

But then, where would we all be if the castle hadn't been protected and the dragons hadn't been bound?

Magic coursed out of the wall and through me. I felt big, strong, and capable. The weight of the entire castle settled on my shoulders. I stood tall, squaring those shoulders.

I felt the burning imprint of the book on my palms.

"I won't disappoint you," I told all those former Wrays.

Then I, Darling Wray Fortune, Guardian of the Castle, floated down the corridor, buoyed by my new sense of responsibility, and wafted into the wardrobe hall.

"Darling?" Lindy asked. "Are you ill?"

I ground to a halt, fingers curled as if I still held the book. The wardrobe hall was almost crowded. Lindy and Marci were there; so were Princess Mariposa and Selma the Head Laundress. The silver-gray dress the Princess had worn a couple of days earlier lay in damp folds over the desk.

"I'm great," I said.

Lindy frowned, but the Head Laundress gestured to the dress's collar.

"I didn't realize a jewel was still pinned to the dress when I laundered it," Selma said.

"Oh my," Princess Mariposa said, fingering the large rent in the bodice's front.

"That's a terrible rip," Lindy said.

"I always go over your clothes. I check every pocket," Selma said, eyeing Lindy like a blotch on a freshly washed apron. "Lately, the Laundresses have noticed things messed with, rearranged . . . missing." She arched an eyebrow.

And she thought Lindy was behind it? Was that what the dresses had tried to show me?

"No," Marci burst out. "This is my fault, Your Highness. That dress should never have left my care with any jewel of yours still on it."

"No, ma'am, you mustn't blame Marci!" Selma reddened. "This is my responsibility."

"A pretty dress like that all ruined. And Your Highness's pin lost." Lindy clicked her tongue.

Princess Mariposa's head whipped around.

"My pin is lost?"

"Oh no," Selma piped up, digging in her apron pocket. "I have it. Right here."

The emerald lay facedown in her palm. The gold wire pin on the back was bent. She laid it gently in the Princess's outstretched hand.

Princess Mariposa blinked back tears.

"Was—was it terribly valuable?" Selma said.

The Princess shook her head, folding her fingers around the jewel.

"Was that your mother's?" Marci asked gently.

Princess Mariposa nodded.

"I'll pay for the repair, whatever it costs, if it takes me the rest of my days," Selma said.

"I'll pay!" Marci cried.

"May I see it, Your Highness?" I asked, wiggling between Marci and the Princess. "Please?"

Startled, Princess Mariposa opened her hand. The emerald winked at me in the morning light, and then I noticed the surface was carved in the shape of a butterfly. A thin gold rim surrounded the stone.

"It's beautiful," I said. "Did the Queen give it to you because of your name?"

"When I was sixteen," she said with a catch in her voice.

Marci shook her head, warning me. *Don't upset Her Highness.* She gathered up the dress. "I'll speak to the

Head Seamstress," she said. "I'm sure the bodice can be replaced. Good as new."

Princess Mariposa waved the dress away as if the matter was dismissed. She turned to Selma. "I should have remembered to remove the pin. We'll say no more about this."

Selma bobbed a curtsy. "Thank you, Your Majesty. It will never happen again," she said.

"I'm sure it won't," the Princess agreed. "It never has before."

Lindy nodded as if that was a satisfactory end to the matter. She'd always taken the greatest care with Her Majesty's clothes. She might get annoyed with the Laundresses, but damage the Princess's dress? Never.

Throwing one last look at Lindy, Selma left. Marci carefully folded the dress into a parcel.

Princess Mariposa glanced down at her palm.

"The jeweler can repair that," Marci commented. "I can have it sent down to the city today."

Princess Mariposa turned the pin over in her hand, considering. Then she held the pin out to me.

"Thank you, Marci, but I can't part with it. Darling, take this to my room and place it in the tray on my bedside table."

"As you wish," Marci replied.

"Yes, Your Highness," I said. I took the pin and curtsied.

Lindy eyed me; I was not to dally. I hurried off to the Princess's bedroom.

I paused at the bedroom door, savoring the moment. I, Darling *Wray* Fortune, Princess's Girl, was carrying one of Her Highness's prized jewels. I glanced down at the emerald pin, expanding it in my mind.

Not just any jewel. No. This was the treasured Heart of the Forest. Long ago, a powerful enchantress poured all her love for the Mountain King into the gem. But the Mountain King did not love the enchantress in return, so he cast her gift deep into the caves under the mountain. There it languished, burning with its emerald light of true love. How the mountain ached with that stone buried in its depths! It rolled the gem in soil and pushed it up, inch by inch, foot by foot, year after year, until it finally expelled the jewel onto a sunlit path by a mountain stream.

I grinned. I couldn't wait to tell Gillian that story. I'd add a big finale. . . . I clicked my tongue, considering. The story needed the right heroine to find the jewel. Ah, a goat girl with an ailing mother! Perfect. I opened the door and sailed in.

The Princess's bedroom was as she'd left it. The bed curtains of royal-purple velvet lined in blue satin hung untied. A coverlet of blue satin embroidered with purple-and-gold butterflies lay tousled at the foot of the bed. Lace-trimmed silk pillows were scattered on the floor.

A dressing gown had been flung over a panel of the head-board, which rose in great carved heights under the canopy. A half-empty crystal goblet waited at a marble-topped bedside table.

"What are you doing in here?" Francesca asked, brandishing a feather duster.

"I am on an errand for Her Highness," I proclaimed, producing the jewel with a flourish.

"Well," she said, "get on with it."

It was then I noticed that Francesca wore a long string of the Princess's pearls draped around her neck. She'd been standing before a tall mirror over a fancy table topped with a bowl of roses. A grin broke out on my face.

Francesca had been playing dress-up with the Princess's jewels! And I'd caught her doing it.

"Are you tidying up the room?" I asked. "Do the pearls help you?"

Francesca flung the feather duster over her shoulder and clutched at the pearls, wide-eyed with horror. The feather duster bounced on the table and glanced off the bowl of roses. A cascade of petals fluttered to the floor. Startled, Francesca trod on the petals, releasing their scent into the air.

"I—I—I—" Francesca sputtered.

I chuckled. She'd pulled a lot of mean tricks on me, and now I had something on her. I waltzed over to the bedside table and laid the pin on the tray there. Another day, I might have tapped the tray with a finger to hear the crystal chime. But not today! I turned around. Francesca was on her hands and knees, scrambling to collect the fallen rose petals.

"Now, Francesca," I said, "do be sure to do a thorough job of Her Majesty's room. And *do* clean off those pearls before you put them back."

Francesca gasped, dropping her fistful of petals to grab the necklace and examine it. Realizing there was nothing wrong with it, she jumped up.

"If you breathe one word, I'll—"

"Yes? You'll what?"

"I'll—"

"Be in big trouble? Look silly in front of the other Girls?"

"You—you—" she gasped.

"Lose your place as Head Girl? What? Come on, what?"

Francesca took a step toward me, balling her fists at her sides. Patches of red danced on her cheeks. Her eyes darkened to coal.

"I'll have my mother find a reason to get rid of you," she said.

Behind me the headboard creaked, and I had the feeling that eyes were boring into the back of my head. *Ghosts?* I glanced over my shoulder.

Despite my eerie sense of being watched, nothing was there.

I turned my attention back to Francesca.

Could the Head Housekeeper find a reason to get rid of me? A part of me thought not; I was the Princess's favorite—she took *me* to the Royal Cemetery, not Francesca. She'd introduced me as her friend, not Francesca. But if she found out about the dresses ... I'd have to see to it that that didn't happen.

"Be careful—those petals could stain the rug," I said, strolling toward the door. "And don't worry. Your little secret is safe with me."

14

With my new sense of importance, I took extra care over my work, keeping one eye on Lindy and one on the wrinkled handkerchief before me. Lindy whistled as she whisked her iron over a petticoat. If she had a guilty conscience, it didn't show. I'd suspected her wrongly before, I remembered with a twinge. When I'd thought she was plotting against the Princess, she'd been sneaking off to meet her boyfriend, Captain Bryce. She might have a bit of a temper, but she wasn't mean.

Whoever had fiddled around in the Laundresses' domain, it wasn't Lindy.

Forty-Nine had insisted I go down to the under-cellar. And I had. But since then, I'd been too involved in my own search for answers. I'd neglected the problem the dresses wanted me to solve. I folded the handkerchief neatly and added it to my pile of finished work.

"Here," Lindy said, holding out a camisole. "See what you can do with this."

Lindy never let me touch the Princess's clothes. And I couldn't help thinking about how sore she'd been because I'd touched up that sleeve.

"Really?" I said.

"Sure." She grinned. "Aren't I training you to take over for me someday?"

I smiled so big my ears nearly met at the back of my head. I took the delicate silk garment and laid it over my ironing board. Then I picked up my water bottle and sprinkled it. Then gently, as if the camisole were a baby, I smoothed it with my hot iron.

Lindy spoke over my shoulder. "Press each ribbon separately. One quick pass, don't loll around about it."

"Okay," I said, pressing the lavender ribbons one at a time. Did all Princesses wear such fancy underclothes? I grinned, imagining Dulcie howling over such a camisole.

No doubt ribbons would itch as badly as her winter clothes did.

"Okay, just tickle that lace, don't scorch it!"

"Yes, ma'am," I said, tracing the lace trim with the tip of my iron.

When I was finished, Lindy held the camisole up for inspection.

"Didn't I know you'd be my best Under-presser ever?" she asked. "Didn't I pick you out special?"

Actually, Marci had shoved me into this job, but I wasn't about to remind Lindy of that.

"Finish up there and take the afternoon off," she told me as she returned to her ironing board.

"Yes, ma'am!"

She hadn't given me a whole afternoon off in ages. My irons fairly sizzled as I whipped them over my work. I pressed and folded so fast it nearly made me dizzy. As soon as I finished, I headed for the closet. I'd rescue Lindy from Selma's wrath! I'd find out who was bothering the Laundresses.

I reached out for the closet doorknob when I heard someone behind me.

"Darling," Marci said, "shouldn't you be working?"

"I have the afternoon off." I let go of the knob and turned around. "Lindy said so."

Marci jingled the keys on her chatelaine.

"That so? Then you should run along," she said.

I'd have to go to the under-cellar and investigate without a dress.

I sighed dramatically to let her know what a valiant

sacrifice I was making and stomped off. The castle had too many bosses. You couldn't take two steps without tripping over one. I marched down the back stair and along the corridor to the kitchens.

Mrs. Pepperwhistle stood inside the Soup Chef's room. She held her leather-bound housekeeper's book in her hand.

"A little less pepper," she told him. Then she saw me. "Are you where you should be?"

"Lindy gave me the afternoon off," I said.

Mrs. Pepperwhistle regarded me silently for a moment. "Very well," she replied.

I skipped on down the corridor, stopping at the Pastry Chef's room on the chance that he might need a taster.

A Scullery Maid brandished a broom at me.

"Don't put one foot on this here floor," she said. "I've cleaned it three times today."

"I'm sorry," I said, trying to appear sympathetic while looking for the Pastry Chef. "Why so many?"

"This morning there was sawdust tracked about. Sawdust! I've never seen the like. And then someone—I'm not naming names—spilled a jar of cream, and what a mess! And now, half a crock of flour. Whoosh! Everywhere!" She paused, panting. "If one more person makes a mess on this floor—"

"I was passing by," I said quickly, and ducked out the doorway.

Clearly, the under-cellar was the only safe spot in the castle.

A noisy clatter greeted me as I stepped off the stair. Pots clanged as they changed hands from Under-scrubbers to Under-dryers. The slap of paddles churning clothes in washing vats. The squish of clothes running through the wringer. The splash of water all around. A faint whistle of steam rising off the hearths. Everyone was hard at work.

I gravitated toward the laundry. The dresses had disguised me as a Laundress, so it seemed like a good place to start. I wove through the laundry stations, nodding at the Laundresses with a neighborly air and keeping a sharp lookout for anything unusual.

It would help if I knew what I was looking for. Why would someone mess about in the laundry? *I* wouldn't tangle with a Laundress armed with her heavy wooden paddle. I stepped on a sliver of soap and slid across the floor, arms flailing, kicking up sawdust.

"Don't get any of that in my vat!" Ursula warned, eyeing me as if I needed a good scrubbing.

"Sorry," I said.

I bent over to pick up the soap and spotted a glimmer. Squatting down, I dug through the soft, crumbly sawdust that the Laundresses laid down to soak up the excess moisture. My fingers grazed a hard lump. Grasping it, I yanked it free. It was a half-empty saltshaker. Maybe whoever was causing trouble in the laundry worked in the kitchens?

"What's this doing here?" I exclaimed, holding it up.

"Give me that!" Ursula padded over to me.

I dropped the saltshaker into her outstretched palm. She squinted at it.

"That must have come from the kitchens," I said, seizing on my chance to exonerate Lindy.

"Selma is going to hear about this," Ursula muttered. Then she thrust it into her apron pocket and shook a finger in my face. "Go play somewhere else, Darling. We have work to do."

"I wasn't playing," I protested.

"No? What were you doing?" she demanded.

I didn't bother to answer her. I dusted the sawdust off my hands. What a day! I, Darling *Wray* Fortune, had solved the Laundresses' problem, satisfied the dresses' demands, and still had time left over. I skipped off. My foot struck something solid in the sawdust. I felt it bounce off the toe of my boot.

But I hurried on, not stopping to see what it was.

15

"New stockings," Jane said over the rumble of kitchen chatter. She handed me a lavender ball.

Marci sighed as she leaned toward the crackling fire. The three of us sat wedged in a toasty corner, ignoring the envious glances of latecomers. The Head Cook sat at the end of the table, sorting a pile of recipes.

I'd spent the late afternoon in the stables, watching Roger polish tack. Running in and out of the castle had left me windburned and cold. Now, stuffed with a hot supper and basking in the fire's glow, I was ready to wheedle answers out of Jane.

But first, I unrolled the stockings to admire them. Elaborate cable stitching decorated the sides.

"I love them!" I told her, beaming. "Thank you."

"That's lovely work, Jane," Marci commented.

Jane blushed, her blurry blue eyes sparkling. "Nothing, just a time passer."

"Didn't Francesca give you mittens?" Marci asked, eyeing my chapped hands.

"No," I said. Why hadn't I thought to ask her for them?

Jane's eyes flashed. "Upper-servants! I have half a mind to speak to Mrs. Pepperwhistle about this."

"You should knit her some," Marci said. "Some *fancy* mittens."

"The Girls' mittens have velvet cuffs," the Head Cook pointed out, choosing that moment to chime in. "Silver-gray with pewter buttons."

Jane turned to her. "Do they now?" Then she nudged me in the ribs. "You should have said so sooner."

"Sorry," I said, anxious to turn the conversation in my direction. "So I was wondering—"

Gillian appeared across the room, joking around with the other Under-dryers. Steam rose off their aprons as they wormed their way closer to the hearth. One of the Cooks vigorously batted away the steam as if the air around her was aflame.

"Can you get buttons for me?" Jane asked Marci.

"—about my mother," I said.

"I'll ask the Head Seamstress," Marci told her, and then looked at me. "What about your mother?"

Jane pursed her lips, ready to repeat her favorite phrase: *she was a sweet, kind person.*

"Why'd she marry my father?" I blurted out. "If he was a good-for-nothing?"

"You shouldn't repeat unpleasant gossip," Jane retorted.

"As I recall," Marci said, "he was handsome and charming. A spinner of tales."

Jane glowered at Marci.

"About what?" I asked, eager to learn more.

"Oh, adventure, the sea, the Indigo Isles ... treasure," Marci mused. "Your mother had a small inheritance. He convinced her to invest it in his new venture."

"That's about enough," Jane said.

"He swept her off her feet," the Head Cook added. "She married him before she had time to think about what she was doing."

Jane's cheeks burned.

"And?" I urged.

"He sailed away." Marci studied her hands. "Later, we had word that pieces of wreckage had surfaced off a cove north of the kingdom."

"He would have come back," Jane interrupted. "They'd have been happy."

"We hoped so," the Head Cook said quietly, "but now we'll never know."

Gillian wove her way to us, waving good-bye to her friends.

"I'm here for a story," Gillian said.

"Some things never change," Marci replied, glancing at me.

I pictured a pretty blond woman waving good-bye to a sailing ship. The woman seemed like someone in a story, not like a real mother. But then I'd never known my mother, so it was hard to imagine her.

"Yes, well, I thought *you* could tell me if there are stories about the castle being haunted, seeing how you've lived here for ages," Gillian said with a wide-eyed, innocent smile that didn't fool Marci a bit.

"But what about—" I said, eager to pry more details out of Marci.

"Hauntings!" the Head Cook exclaimed. "Nothing like a roaring fire on a wintry night for a good ghost story!"

A collective *oooh* resonated through the room.

Marci adjusted the mauve scarf knotted under her collar, eyeing Gillian like a flame that needed quenching.

"Oh, Marci," Jane said, straightening up. "Tell them about the ghost in the tower."

I frowned at her.

"Ghost in the tower!" Gillian breathed. "Oh my."

"Marci was already telling me a story." I poked her in the ribs.

"Did it involve ghosts?" Gillian said, poking me back.

The whole group stared at me as if to say *Shut up before you ruin our chance to hear this story.*

"No," I said, wilting.

"Then be quiet and listen," Marci began. "Years ago, an old woman lived in the south tower of the castle. She'd been a lady once, beautiful and rich, but over the years, her fortunes turned. She'd lost her lands, her title, and, ultimately, her looks. She was reduced to sewing for the other ladies of the court."

"How dreadful," Gillian said. "And then she died?"

"Are you telling this story?" Marci asked in a steely tone.

Gillian shook her head, lips sealed.

"Soon her fingers became gnarled and she could no longer sew. The Head Housekeeper felt sorry for her and gave her a room with the Cooks. The Head Cook set a place for her in the kitchens every evening. One little servant girl washed her clothes and saw to her needs. But she was very proud and ashamed of her poverty."

"Sounds like them court people," a Footman chimed in.

"She withdrew to a room high in the south tower, in an area that had fallen into disuse. There she lived, bent and twisted, creeping down only for meals. The servants begged her to come back, but she refused. Over time, she developed a rattling cough and grew increasingly ill. The little servant girl who washed her clothes procured medicine for her, digging into her own pockets to pay for it. She went up to the tower, medicine in hand."

Marci paused, massaging her wrist. I knew she was waiting for someone to beg for more.

"And?" the Head Cook prompted.

"And the old woman had vanished."

The fire crackled in the grate, shooting sparks upward. The flickering light played over Marci's hair. The darkness in the kitchen's corners seemed to crouch with bated breath. I leaned forward, drawn into the story.

"No one had seen the old woman come down from the tower. Her possessions were all in her room. The servants heard an eerie moaning and followed the sound, thinking the old woman had wandered to some other part of the tower and had fallen or been injured."

The log in the fire snapped. Gillian jumped.

"They searched the entire tower, high and low, but the old woman had disappeared without a trace."

"Do you think she's still up there?" Gillian said.

"Afterward, on several occasions, a ghost was seen walking the passages of the south tower. A pale specter holding out a hand, like someone groping their way through a maze." Marci lowered her voice to a whisper. "And the question remains: what became of the old woman? How did she vanish into thin air?"

"Did your grandmother tell you that story?" Gillian asked.

Marci nodded. "She knew the old woman well."

"Maybe it was some other ghost, not the old woman," Gillian supplied. "Who would know? Ghosts all look alike."

"Ghosts and more ghosts, why not a whole platoon?" the Footman asked.

"I don't hold with medicine, myself," the Head Cook said, shuffling her recipes. "A nice chicken broth, that's the cure for what ails you."

I shivered in the darkness. Wind howled against the windows, rattling the panes. Icy cold bit the tip of my nose. I pulled my blankets closer to my chin. Thoughts chased around inside my skull. My mother sobbing over the loss of her sailor. The old woman haunting the south tower.

Roger and I had seen a ghost. A real, actual, live ghost?

No, ghosts weren't alive. They were dead . . . which meant—I refused to think about what it meant. No. I would think about my poor sobbing mother and my poor *dead* sailor father. . . .

I rolled over. It was late, and it was best that I should go straight to sleep.

Unfortunately, I rolled in the direction of the dormitory door. It just so happened that the door chose that moment to *creak* open. And a vague, tall, whitish shape flowed into the room.

My every nerve tingled. Every hair on my arms rose. Dread pooled in my stomach. Every muscle tensed, waiting for the ghost to glide its way over to my bed. Was it the ghost of that old woman? I gritted my teeth, transfixed by the sight of it. It glided over to Francesca's bed.

Part of me thought that I should scream or jump up or *do* something. The rest of me lay frozen in fear. A soft sound grazed my ear. A quiet *sch-pop* coming from the direction of Francesca's bed.

Then the ghost turned in my direction.

What I should have done at the moment, I didn't do. My eyes slapped shut, and my entire being pretended to sleep, willing the ghost to leave me alone. *Please go away.*

I heard a rustling sound, a soft scraping, and then silence. I squeezed my eyes shut and counted my heart-beats. Why didn't it leave? There was a whole castle full of people to haunt. Why did it have to come here?

After what seemed like a century, I heard the door open and close.

It was then that my senses returned to me. What was I thinking? A real, actual ghost had come into *my* dormitory and I'd let it? Just like that?

I sat straight up, flinging the covers off. I, Darling Wray Fortune, was no coward!

The freezing night air gripped me like a Laundress wringing out a wet towel. All the breath *whoosh*ed from my lungs. Shivering, I slid out of bed and wiggled into my slippers. I wished I had a candle or a lantern, but if the ghost could get around in the dark, so could I.

I crept across the room and inched the door open. Down the corridor, a glimmer of white swayed in the cold air.

Aha! I crept after it, clenching my jaw to keep my teeth from chattering. The moon had set, and the darkness in the corridor was such that I could barely see my slippers. The ghost coasted down the corridor and toward a stair. There it hovered, and I stopped in my tracks, holding my breath. It slid down the steps, and I waited a few moments before I tiptoed to the top of the stairs. The ghost sailed away below me, down another corridor.

Where was it going? I hurried after it, my slippers soundless on the marble. The ghost drifted in the direction of the Princess's rooms. I always went into her room from either the pressing room or the wardrobe hall, but there were fancy gilded doors in the main corridor that Her Highness used. And the ghost headed toward them.

I stopped at the nearest corner and hid behind it. I snuck a peek at the ghost down the corridor. It hovered in front of the doors. My heart skipped a beat. It didn't mean to hurt the Princess, did it? Could it? It had moved my ribbon. Sliding a ribbon around the castle was one thing; doing someone real harm was another. I clenched my fists.

If the ghost slid through the Princess's doors, I'd have to pound on them to wake her up.

I had no idea what I'd say when she answered her door. *Excuse me, Your Highness, for disturbing you, but a vicious ribbon-swiping ghost was headed your way.* I ground my teeth; how much trouble was I about to get into?

The ghost hung there, glimmering in the dim passage, twisting slightly as if uncertain what it wanted to do. Then it turned back around. Could ghosts see? Hear? Smell? I was afraid that I was about to find out. I held my breath, too frightened to run away.

And then it slipped around again and wafted to the end of the passage. I felt a sudden breeze, and then the ghost vanished.

At that moment, I wished fervently that I'd brought Iago. I could have sent him scurrying down to the end of the passage to check up on the ghost. But I hadn't; I'd been too busy being brave.

I stood, trying to scrounge up the nerve to stroll down there and see what I could discover, but my burst of bravery had melted away. I shook so hard that my knees knocked together. My teeth chattered. My flannel night-gown crackled with cold. I felt frozen in place. The only warm parts of me were my slippered feet. Which, thankfully, woke up and began to walk, moving me away from the corridor and any contact with ghosts.

I decided that tackling ghosts was best left to Roger.

Except, my conscience murmured, when they threatened the Princess. Not that that had happened; maybe the ghost had gotten lost. After all, it was a big castle with lots of corridors. Yes, that was it. The ghost was confused. Maybe it was really old and had trouble remembering.

I consoled myself with that thought as I hastened back to my warm bed.

16

The next morning I woke up tangled in my covers like a fly in a spider's web. I scrambled my way out into the morning, which was bright with sunshine. I climbed up on my bed and looked out the window. Icicles hung in a row from the sill. The world beyond was one of those blinding-bright winter days that look warmer than they are. A glistening river of snow rolled over the lawns below. My breath fogged the glass. I wrote my name in the mist before it disappeared.

"You can write?" Dulcie asked, squinting at the window.

"Sure," I said, hopping down onto the braided rug beside my bed. "Can't you?"

She shook her head.

Francesca shuffled over to us, hair in a snarl, eyes bleary.

"What were you writing?" she snapped.

Dulcie ducked into her clothes. I eyed Francesca.

"Secrets," I said, grinning.

"What secrets?" she said.

"If I told you, it wouldn't be secret."

Her eyes narrowed; she glanced at Dulcie, who was studiously buttoning her dress.

"Can't read," Dulcie volunteered.

I retrieved my clothes from their hook. It was too cold to stand around in a nightgown while Francesca glowered at me.

"You better not have any secrets," she said at last.

"Everybody does," Ann said from across the room.

"I know Ann's," another Girl sang out.

"No, you don't," Ann said, throwing a rolled-up sock at the other Girl.

"Does this secret have a name?" Kate giggled.

Ann blushed.

"Get dressed," Francesca said, evidently deciding that secrets weren't a subject she cared to discuss.

She marched over to her bed and began pulling on her clothes.

Ann stuck her tongue out at Kate.

Muffled noises sounded outside the dormitory. A short Kitchen Maid came in, holding the door open for a taller Maid, who lugged our heavy breakfast tray into the room. Behind her a distant shout echoed down the hall.

"Good morning, Girls," the tall Maid called, putting our tray down on the side table.

Dulcie popped up, eager to grab a jelly-filled pastry. She snatched up the gooiest selection every morning, as if she couldn't wait to muss up her clean clothes.

"What is all that racket?" Kate asked the Maids.

"Some to-do," the tall Maid confided, eyes shining. "Her Highness has half the castle astir over it."

"Over what?" Francesca sniffled as she tied her apron.

The tall Maid took a breath, ready to spill whatever juicy tidbits she had, but the short Maid spoke first.

"They don't tell us anything in the kitchens. Ask your mother what's what," she said.

"I will." Francesca reached for her boots.

"The Head Steward is up, and I saw the Head Cook running about in her dressing gown!" the tall Maid said, twisting her hands together, unable to contain herself. "You don't suppose it's a war?"

"War!" Francesca scoffed. "If it was something like that, the Guards would be out, not the Head Steward."

"Isn't the Head Cook in the kitchen cooking?" Dulcie asked, nabbing her roll.

The short Maid shook her head. "She doesn't do little things like breakfast. She oversees the big meals."

"It must be some calamity," the tall Maid persisted.

Shaking her head, Francesca shoved her right foot into her boot. She screamed and snatched her foot back out again. The boot dropped with a clatter. She clutched her toes.

"Something bit me," she hollered. A dot of blood oozed up through her sock.

"Was it a spider?" another Girl asked, turning pale.

Several Girls froze, hairbrushes in hand.

"Spider?" one squeaked.

"It's too cold for spiders," Francesca snarled, grabbing the boot.

"Is it a snake?" one cried.

"A mouse?" another guessed.

I flinched; they'd blame Iago if they knew he was under my bed.

Francesca upended her boot and shook it.

Something tumbled onto the braided rug beneath her. Francesca's face drained of all color; her lips whitened. The Girls surged forward; one grabbed a pillow to combat whatever creature lay there. They gasped in unison.

I scrambled over them to get a look.

There, glinting in the winter-morning sunshine, was Princess Mariposa's emerald pin.

The Girls clustered around Francesca, a mix of wonder, surprise, and outrage on their faces. Francesca sat, boot in hand, staring in horror at the incriminating flash of green nestled in the rug.

"What is that?" Kate asked.

"Jewels," Ann breathed.

"Oh my goodness," the tall Kitchen Maid exclaimed, clasping her hands to her cheeks.

"Thief!" the other Maid cried.

Francesca's boot hit the wooden floor with a *thunk*. "I didn't put that in there!" Francesca exclaimed.

"Where'd it come from?" a Girl wondered.

"Whose is it?" Dulcie asked nobody in particular.

"I've seen the Princess wearing it," Ann said.

"We have to get the Head Steward!" the short Maid said.

"We have to find the Head Housekeeper," the other added.

They goggled at each other and dived for the door. They nearly fell over each getting through it.

Mrs. Pepperwhistle swept into the dormitory, flanked by her henchwomen: the Head Duster, the Head Polisher, and the Head Sweeper. We Girls stood at the foot of our beds, having jumped into our clothes and put our hair in order as fast as we could. Ann's cheeks bulged with the pastry she was gobbling down. Mrs. Pepperwhistle arched a prim eyebrow at her, and she swallowed the rest whole.

I hadn't eaten breakfast. My stomach ached. I had just put that pin on the table next to Her Highness's bed yesterday. Now it lay on Francesca's rug.

And I knew how it had gotten there.

"Where was it found?" Mrs. Pepperwhistle asked, picking up the pin.

"In my boot," Francesca answered, pale and straight. Her apron bow sat perfectly centered at her back. Face scrubbed. Boots tied. Hair braided.

"And how did it happen to be there?" Mrs. Pepperwhistle asked.

"I don't know," Francesca said. "The last time I saw it was yesterday, when Darling put it on the Princess's bedside table."

"Is that true, Darling?"

"Yes, ma'am. The pin had been damaged in the laundry. Her Highness asked me to put it in her room," I said.

Francesca gave me a pleading glance.

"Francesca was dusting the Princess's room; she saw me," I added.

That wasn't all she'd been doing, but now didn't seem like a good time to mention her toying with strings of priceless pearls. Francesca might play around, but she wouldn't *take* something of the Princess's. The ghost had moved it. Why, I couldn't imagine, but it had gone and stuck the jewel in Francesca's boot!

"Were any other Girls in the Princess's rooms yesterday?" Mrs. Pepperwhistle asked.

"Maybe Darling went back later and picked it up," Francesca said. "She has access to all rooms while she works."

So much for not tattling on her.

"No, I didn't!" I roared. "Ask Lindy."

Mrs. Pepperwhistle frowned. "Her Highness woke this morning and was quite distressed to discover the pin gone."

"Stolen, she said," the Head Polisher added.

"Put your foot up," Mrs. Pepperwhistle said to her daughter. Francesca lifted her booted foot, and her mother ran her finger around the laced rim. "Too tight for the pin to have fallen in accidentally while she was cleaning the Princess's rooms. Someone put it in there."

She straightened up and walked down the row of Girls, looking at each one of us.

"Does anyone have anything to say?"

We shook our heads.

"Ladies," she said to her assistants, "search each Girl's things. Be thorough."

My heart fluttered. The only thing I had was the box stamped ARTICHOKES, and Iago and his family were in there. What would happen to them? The Head House-keeper didn't tolerate mice. They were friends to me, but to her they were vermin.

I felt woozy as, one by one, each Girl's trunk or box was hauled out and searched. Several had candy or cake, which was against the rules, and the Head Duster was quick to confiscate it. One had a packet of letters tied up with a pink ribbon. These were slipped into Mrs. Pepperwhistle's pocket for later discussion with the guilty Girl.

I caught a couple of Girls smirking. *Ann's love letters,* one mouthed.

I didn't care if every Girl had a stack of love letters and a basketful of muffins hidden in her things. All I cared about were my mice.

Finally, Mrs. Pepperwhistle's assistants reached my bed and yanked out my box. As they flipped the lid off, I gripped the bedpost to keep from falling over.

"What is this?" the Head Sweeper exclaimed.

I turned to look, certain that I'd be confronted by a row of tiny frightened black eyes. But Iago had heard the commotion and escaped. Instead, there lay my lavender socks next to the library book, shimmering in all its gilded crimson glory on a bed of sand. Time stopped. My heart refused to beat. My brain refused to think. All I could do was stare at *Magnificent Reflections.*

Mrs. Pepperwhistle swooped up the book as if rescuing it from the rubbish bin.

"What is this doing here?" she demanded.

"I—I borrowed it from the Librarian," I sputtered.

"And you put it under your bed?" she said. "One of Her Majesty's priceless books?"

Francesca stared at the crate, dumbfounded.

"Where did the sand come from?" the Head Polisher demanded.

"Where indeed?" Mrs. Pepperwhistle agreed.

"I found it in my bed every night. I didn't know what else to do with it." I couldn't tell the truth—*Magic mice swept it up, your Head Housekeeperness, and that's where they stowed it. Ask them. They'll tell you.*

"Is that true—sand in her bed?" she demanded of Francesca.

"Um . . . ," Francesca said. Caught without an excuse.

Mrs. Pepperwhistle's mouth hardened into a thin line. "It seems a great deal has been going on around here besides your work, Girls."

The Princess's Girls studied their boots.

"Ann, you'll be in charge today. See to it that all chores are completed promptly. Francesca, you and Darling will wait here until sent for."

"Yes, ma'am," we muttered in unison.

Mrs. Pepperwhistle swept to the door with her henchwomen in her wake. She paused with her hand on the knob. "And, Ann, see to it that something is done about that sand."

And then she strolled out the door with Magnificent's magic-humming book in her hand.

17

Francesca collapsed on her bed. Ann and Kate glanced at each other. Dulcie helped herself to a second pastry. I settled on the edge of my eiderdown, rolling my lavender socks in my hands. Why hadn't I cried out when I'd seen the ghost?

"Do you think they'll both be fired?" someone whispered.

"Take the box out and dump the sand into the rubbish bin," Ann ordered one of the Girls. "And then put it back under Darling's bed."

"Why not throw the whole thing away?" the Girl asked.

I bit my lower lip, determined not to cry.

"Just put it back," Ann said with a sigh.

"But it looks heavy," the Girl whined. "Why drag it back up here?"

I gnawed on my knuckle.

Crimson spots warmed Ann's cheeks. "It's all she has. Put it back, like I said."

A roomful of eyes stared at me, Darling the Poor Girl. The only one with nothing but an old vegetable crate that had a pile of sand, a pair of socks, and a book that didn't belong to her inside it.

"For what it's worth, I'm sorry," Ann offered.

"About the sand—or the glue?" I replied, remembering what they'd done to my hairbrush.

They all shifted uneasily.

"Are you going to tell on us?" Kate asked.

The door opened, and a Footman stuck his head in.

"Francesca and Darling, come with me," he said.

Laying my socks aside, I stood up.

"Where to?" Francesca asked, collecting herself and straightening her apron.

"Her Highness's office," he said.

I walked past clusters of anxious-looking Girls. They were scared I'd talk. Not one of them was worried about what might happen to me—or Francesca. I followed the Footman and Francesca out the door, closing it behind me without a backward glance.

Princess Mariposa's office glittered like the inside of a jewel box. A rich carpet covered the floor. Gilded chairs were scattered about. Gilded picture frames held beautifully painted scenes of forests and pools, bowls of lush fruits, and portraits of royal-looking people. Thick curtains clustered at the tall windows. Fancy little tables displayed gleaming porcelain statuettes.

At the center of it all, behind a gilded desk, Her Highness sat on a gilded chair. She wore an elaborately ruffled dressing gown that tied in a big bow at her throat. Her ebony curls rested about her shoulders. Her face was pale, as if she hadn't had much sleep.

The emerald pin lay on the desk before her, next to my book.

Francesca and I stood, hands clasped behind our backs, trying our best to look innocent. Mrs. Pepperwhistle, Marsdon the Head Steward, Lindy, and Marci were grouped to the side. Lindy glowered at me as if she meant to iron the wickedness right out of me.

"So," the Princess began, "my pin mysteriously appeared in your boot this morning, Francesca."

"Yes, Your Highness," Francesca said.

"And you have no idea how it got there?"

"No." Francesca shook her head.

"No one saw anything? Heard anything?"

We both shook our heads. I decided that no matter what, I wasn't going to mention the ghost.

"You saw Darling put it on my bedside table?"

"Yes, ma'am."

"Was it there when you finished your tidying?"

"Yes."

"Darling, did you reenter my room after Francesca left?"

"No, ma'am."

"She was workin'," Lindy put in.

Princess Mariposa eyed Lindy. "You are certain of that?"

Lindy colored. "Pretty certain."

Her Highness frowned.

"I was there all afternoon. Darling didn't go near your suite," Marci added.

"So, someone snuck into the Girls' dormitory while they were all asleep and put my pin in Francesca's boot. After, of course, sneaking into my suite to get it. Quite an accomplishment, all in one evening."

Lindy, Marci, and Mrs. Pepperwhistle grew pale.

They were in just as much trouble as Francesca and I were! Any one of them could have taken the pin. Not that they had. The ghost did it. But Princess Mariposa didn't know that.

What could I say? *Pardon me, Your Highness, but the ghost has it in for you?*

"Perhaps it was some kind of bizarre accident?" Marsdon suggested.

"Can you explain how such an *accident* could occur?"

"No, Your Majesty, I am at a loss to explain it. Only to say that I have the utmost confidence in my senior servants. Children, however, are known to play pranks."

Princess Mariposa's eyes blazed. "A prank?"

Francesca trembled so hard, I felt *my* sleeve shake.

"I wouldn't!" she cried.

"I see," Princess Mariposa said, picking up the book. She dusted the cover. "Why is there sand on this book?"

Francesca whimpered.

"Darling had sand in the box under her bed." Mrs. Pepperwhistle spoke as if she wished she didn't have to.

"How did sand get in the box under your bed?" the Princess asked.

"I put it there?" That sounded silly, even to me.

Princess Mariposa set the book down and folded her hands on top of it. I had the feeling that she was prepared to sit there until she got answers, no matter how long it took.

"Why did you have sand in the Girls' dormitory?"

My cheek twitched. The truth threatened to pour out of me. I pressed my lips together.

A knowing gleam lit the Princess's eyes.

"Francesca?" she said. "Explain."

"It was a joke," Francesca said in a tiny voice.

"Was Darling amused?"

"No, ma'am." Francesca hung her head.

"Neither am I."

Silence filled the room. A tear trickled down Francesca's chin.

"So you do play pranks, just not on me," the Princess said in a chagrined tone. "Francesca, until we can resolve the matter of my pin in your boot, you are suspended from my service."

Francesca sobbed.

Mrs. Pepperwhistle took a step forward, but the Princess held up a hand to stop her.

"Now then, Darling, why was my book under your bed?"

"I borrowed it from the Librarian; I wanted to read it. I was going to take it back."

"I see." It was obvious from her tone that she didn't. "Shouldn't you have asked my permission first?"

My mouth opened, but nothing came out. It had never occurred to me to ask.

"Am I unkind? Am I such an *ogress* that you felt you couldn't talk to me?"

"Um."

"Is this the sort of behavior I can expect from the last Wray?"

The last Wray. The words drummed in my heart. I'd not only disappointed Her Highness, I'd let down the Wrays.

"Well?" She arched an eyebrow.

"I'm sorry," I said with a sniffle.

"So am I," she replied. "The Librarian handed you this valuable book? For the asking?"

I nodded; it was true and, at the same time, not exactly true.

"I will speak to Master Varick," she said.

My heart fell to my stomach. Marci had warned me. And now I was well and truly caught.

With her mouth set in a grim line, Mrs. Pepperwhistle led a sniveling Francesca away. I almost felt sorry her. Almost. I was too busy ignoring Lindy's glares and Marsdon's disapproving glances. Marci stared at me as if to say, *I told you so.*

Princess Mariposa read through a pile of letters, making a note here or there with her quill pen. Two red spots glowed on her cheeks, betraying her anger.

The door opened and the Footman announced, "Master Varick, Your Majesty's Royal Librarian."

Master Varick surveyed the scene before him, scraping the shock of white hair back from his forehead. He squinted as if the light outside the library was too bright for his eyes. The Princess inclined her head, and the

Librarian jerked into a sudden bow, as if remembering where he was and whom he stood before.

"Did you lend out this book?" she asked, picking it up for him to see.

Master Varick fingered his coat buttons. "Well, yes, I suppose I did."

"You suppose?"

"I did. I remember it clearly."

"And whom did you lend it to?"

"Lady Sara Mallory."

I felt every eye bore into me. Not only was I a liar; I was a thief.

"She usually reads stories, frivolous things; it wasn't like her to want something so serious," Master Varick continued.

The Princess wet her lip with her tongue, considering. "And you never thought to seek my permission before unlocking my father's special collection?"

"I've never received any instructions regarding the collection," Master Varick protested.

Princess Mariposa blanched; evidently that was true. She turned to Marsdon.

"Fetch Lady Sara at once!"

The Head Steward bowed and left with an efficient gleam in his eye.

The ache in my stomach expanded to fill my chest. Should I speak up and tell the Princess about her grandmother's closet? My head popped up, and my mouth fell open. I caught Marci's eye. She held my gaze and then subtly shook her head *no*.

I snapped my mouth closed. If Marci thought I should stay silent, then maybe I should. I gritted my teeth as the door opened again and the Footman spoke.

"Lady Sara Mallory and Mr. Marsdon."

Lady Sara stared in wide-eyed wonder at the gorgeous room and its gorgeous occupant.

"You—you sent for me, Your Highness?"

Lady Sara wore a lavender dress and a silver hair bow. She smiled at Master Varick and then at me. Apparently, she was unaware that she stood next to a notorious criminal.

"A question," Princess Mariposa said. "Did you borrow this book from the library?"

A frown furrowed Lady Sara's smooth brow. "Why, no, Your Highness, it isn't my sort of book!"

"You are sure you didn't?"

"Absolutely sure."

The Princess sat back; this wasn't what she'd been expecting to hear.

"But I lent it to you several days ago!" Master Varick protested.

Lady Sara shook her head. "I'm still making my way

through *Tales Long Ago,* and after that, you promised to mend *Stories Far Away* for me."

"I did mend it," the Librarian grumbled. "It's been waiting for you, but you said you wanted that book." He pointed to the crimson volume.

"I've never even seen that book," Lady Sara exclaimed. "Much less asked for it."

Princess Mariposa cleared her throat. "Is it possible that you've mistaken Darling for Lady Sara?"

Master Varick peered at me as if confronted by a volume of particularly unsavory tales. He unbuttoned his patched coat to reveal an even shabbier waistcoat. He dug a handkerchief out of an inner pocket and proceeded to mop his brow.

"They are about the same size," Marci suggested. "And not far apart in age."

"It's very dark in the library," I said, grabbing onto that like a Stable Boy catching a runaway pony.

"It is!" Lady Sara agreed. "Too much light is bad for books."

"Anybody'd mistake those two in the dark," Lindy put in.

"Maybe so," Marsdon commented, rocking on his heels.

"I know what I saw!" Master Varick shouted, pointing a bony finger at me. "And I've never seen that girl in my life."

Princess Mariposa rubbed her temple. "You're sure it was Lady Sara?"

"Yes, I am."

"And, Lady Sara, you're sure you didn't borrow the book?"

"Oh yes, Your Majesty, quite sure."

"I have a headache," the Princess said, covering her eyes with a pale hand.

18

"Here," Marci said, setting a box of buttons before me. "Sew one of these on each spot that I've marked with a tailor's tack. Just like I taught you."

"Yes, ma'am," I said.

I picked the bodice up off the desk. It shone a soft orange, like a melting sunset. On one side was a long row of neat buttonholes; on the other, a series of Xs marked with white thread. A pile of coral buttons waited in the box. I scooped one up as a sigh escaped me.

"I don't feel sorry for you," Marci said, sorting through her keys.

She didn't, but I did. Across the room, lined up against the wall, were six—count them—*six* baskets full of mending. And I, Darling, had to do it all.

Marci saw my glance. "That's just the beginning. That previous Wardrobe Mistress was as slack as they come. I don't think she did a stitch of mending the whole time she worked here."

Probably not; she was too busy plotting to release the dragons to spend time sewing.

I poked my needle into the first X.

Lindy stalked into the wardrobe hall, pulling an awestruck Gillian along behind her.

"No dawdling," Lindy snapped at her. "There's a pack of work, and you've got to start from scratch." She watched me mournfully.

I threaded a coral button onto my needle as if this required a monumental amount of concentration.

"Oh," Gillian gasped. "I really get to work up here?"

"After you're suitably dressed," Marci said.

Lindy favored Gillian's canvas apron and brown dress with a frown.

"She looks fine; it's not like she's stayin'. This will all be back to normal in a day or two," Lindy exclaimed. "Right, Darlin'?"

"They made me come up here," Gillian said. "I'm not trying to steal your job."

"I know," I told her.

The thread made a slithering sound as it ran through

the bodice fabric. Would it be a day or two? I had my doubts. Princess Mariposa had been so upset by her missing-and-recovered pin and the discovery of the library book that she'd gone back to bed.

And stayed there for three days.

The Head Cook had said that the betrayal of one's servants cut like the sharpest knife—a comment I hadn't found all that helpful, especially since the sentiment was shared by most of the Under-servants. If they viewed Francesca with suspicion, they saw me as a traitor. By taking that book, I'd stepped over a line. They half expected an Upper-servant to do wrong, but one of their own?

It was inexcusable.

"But I borrowed it!" I protested for the thousandth time.

Jane's incessant sobbing didn't help matters. The Under-servants eyed me with a disapproval bordering on affront. Lines were lines, and you knew better than to cross them. Taking—borrowing—one of Her Highness's own books? Well, it wasn't something a good servant would do.

What business did Darling have with a *book*?

Lindy had rallied to my defense. She protested my innocence—not to mention, my outstanding pressing—to anyone who would listen. But to no avail.

"It's out of my hands," Marsdon had said.

The Princess had left no instructions that I was to be fired, but in light of my alleged misdeeds, I would not be returning to my position. Something else would have to be done with me. For a while it looked as though I would be headed out of the castle for good. I heard murmurings about the orphanage.

That's when Marci volunteered to keep an eye on me.

"I'll see to it that she's kept out of trouble," Marci promised in a tone that made me flinch.

Not that I wasn't grateful; I was. But Marci undertook her duty as my keeper with the same relish that the Head Cook lavished on a new dish. She kept me stitching away on my stool, where she could keep an eye on me every minute.

You couldn't accuse Marci of slacking.

"Is that all you have to say?" Marci asked, snapping me out of my reverie.

Gillian bounced on her toes, so excited that she could hardly contain herself. Lindy planted a fist on her hip and tapped her toe.

"Gillian is a hard worker," I told Lindy.

Lindy snorted and hauled Gillian to the pressing room. I scooped up another button. I'd never realized how many buttons, seams, hems, and laces and trims and little bits of decoration were sewn on Her Highness's clothes. And how many of them had come loose or undone. All that dancing and dining and ruling—being a Princess was hard on clothes.

And she had six closets full of them.

"Marci," Princess Mariposa said from the dressing room door, "can I get your opinion of these swatches?"

My heart quivered; the Princess didn't look at me, but she clutched the door like a shield. I had disappointed her. I felt like a rat.

"Yes, Your Highness," Marci replied, hurrying to the door. "What are you ordering?"

I peeked through the open door and saw fabric squares in mouthwatering colors strewn about the carpet.

"Oh, a few things for winter, dresses for court, balls, that sort of thing." Princess Mariposa sighed. "Such a lot of bother," she added as the door swung shut.

I scooped up another button. It glimmered in my hand like a jewel. Like something sewn on one of the hundred dresses. I heard a subtle whistle from the Queen's closet. Lyric was in there, banished during the reign of Her Majesty's headache and yet to be returned. There were piles of samples to sort through. . . . Marci would be busy for half an hour, easily.

I crept over to the pressing room and snuck a look. Lindy stood over Gillian with a hot iron, demonstrating. Baskets of clean laundry waited to be pressed.

I dashed to the closet and popped inside.

"We have to get that ghost!" I told the dresses.

Lyric ruffled his feathers. He cocked his head. The dresses shifted on their hangers uneasily.

"Well, are you with me?"

Silence. If the dresses were capable of being disinterested, they were then. I ground my teeth together. Marci would be distracted for only so long.

"Don't you care about what happens to me?" I asked, angry. "Or the Princess?"

Eighty-Three flapped a grape-colored sleeve toward the window.

The sun shone, painting the yellow of the glass canary at its center on the rose-strewn rug. Shadows scattered to the far corners of the closet.

Lyric bobbed his head.

"Ghosts don't come out in the day," I said, understanding.

The closet door opened. Marci stood there.

"What are you doing?"

"Nothing," I said. "Feeding the canary." I'd fed the canary earlier that morning.

She pointed in the direction of the stool. Shoulders slumped, I trudged back to my spot and plopped down.

Marci settled behind her desk and laced her fingers together. "Don't lie to me," she said. "I don't appreciate it."

"Sorry."

"Let's get a few things straight," she said. "One, I am not your enemy. Two, you got yourself into this mess, and you'll have to get yourself back out again."

"I know."

"Three, you should avoid getting in any more trouble than you're already in."

I picked up a button. I knew *that*.

"Four," she said, with particular emphasis, "the Princess has a guest in the castle, a harpist who will play this evening for Her Highness's enjoyment."

"That's nice," I muttered.

"It is," Marci agreed. "Even more so because all the Head Servants are invited to attend."

"*You're* invited to join the court?"

Marci favored me with a sour glance. "The servants will gather in the minstrels' gallery above the ballroom."

"Oh."

"I expect the concert will last for some time," she finished, taking out her pincushion and scissors. "It will be *very* widely attended, I'm sure. The halls will be practically empty."

"*Oh,*" I said with a smile.

"Get to work," Marci ordered as if she hadn't said anything else.

19

Gillian, Roger, and I crouched over our dinners in a corner of the kitchens. The chatter around us centered on the evening's concert. Even those who weren't invited to attend quivered with excitement.

"Ooh, she's supposed to play just like the fairies," cooed a Kitchen Maid at a nearby table. "All romantic-like. They say people fall in love just by listening!"

"Then they better be careful about who they sit by," Roger said.

Gillian giggled, her dimples deepening.

"Yeah," I agreed, relieved that they were still willing to eat with me.

Earlier, a row of Laundresses had scooted together so

that the open spot on their bench disappeared before I could sit down. And a group of Under-dusters had pointedly avoided my table as if roast weasel were being served there. But Gillian and Roger had shown up and saved me from eating alone. Again.

Eventually, the Under-servants would forgive me. Or I hoped they would. But that would happen a lot faster if I could prove I hadn't put the pin in Francesca's boot or swiped the library book from Lady Sara.

"So," Gillian said, "what is the story with this book you stole?"

"I didn't steal it!" I stabbed my potato with my fork. "I borrowed it from the library."

Roger studied me over his glass of milk. I could see thoughts percolating in his brain. He knew I was telling the truth; he'd seen me with the book—or he'd seen me as Lady Sara with the book.

"What did you want with that book anyway?" he asked.

"It's about my family. I only wanted to read it."

"It's too bad you won't get to. It's probably full of adventures, battles, great love stories, and everything," Gillian said.

I shrugged like it wasn't a big deal. But it was. I could picture it in my hands and feel the magic rising out of it. It wasn't just a book—it was a depository. Knowledge and magic: the very essence of the Wrays themselves simmered between its covers. I'd lost hold of it, and it didn't seem likely that I would get it back.

"Do you think Francesca took that pin?" Roger asked in a low voice.

"No." I glanced over my shoulder to make sure no one was listening. Then I told them about following the ghost. "It had to have done it," I finished. "No one else could have."

"I dunno," Roger said, scratching his head. "Ghosts don't carry things around; they're dead, and they're filmy like fog."

"I've been asking around," Gillian said. "And the Pickers say there's this rare kind of ghost called a polterghost or something like that. And it throws things. Maybe this ghost picks things up and then throws them in boots?"

Roger frowned, thinking this over.

"The thing is," I said, "how do we prove it? How do we catch a ghost?"

"Why would we want to catch it?" Gillian asked, scooping up a bite of carrots.

"To show everyone it's real," Roger added with a nod. "Everyone thinks Darling is behind this, but if we can catch the ghost, they'll all see she's not."

Catch the ghost. The ghost could be anywhere at any

time. It could appear without warning. It put the pin in Francesca's boot; what would it do next?

"Catching the ghost won't explain how she got hold of the book," Gillian said.

"No," Roger agreed. "But if we prove that Darling didn't steal the pin, then more servants will believe that she didn't take the book either."

"Okay. Where do we start looking?" Gillian said, eyes glowing as if *she* thought this would be great fun.

If I were wearing one of the dresses, I'd be disguised. But now, with Gillian along, I couldn't do that. If we found the ghost, it would see us. See *me*.

"The south tower!" Gillian said, pointing her spoon at Roger. "I bet this is that ghost Marci was talking about. And it probably hides in the south tower in between hauntings!"

"I don't think we should go up there," I said, pushing my plate away. My appetite had suddenly disappeared.

"Why not?" Roger asked. "It's as good a place to start as any."

"Afraid of a little bitty ghost?" Gillian asked.

"No," I said, sitting up straighter. "I followed it all alone in the dark, didn't I?"

Roger glanced around. "Soon as the concert gets going, we'll go have a look."

I tried to nod enthusiastically. But failed.

Nobody lived in the south tower. Shorter than the other towers, it looked like an ornament on the front of the castle. It had rooms, of course, and stairs and passageways. But they were cramped and narrow. The ceilings hung low, so you felt the weight of the stones overhead pressing down on you. But it was very pretty from outside, like a plume on a hat.

Now it sat dark and, hopefully, empty. Somewhere an unlatched shutter banged. The wind moaned. At least, I *thought* it was the wind. But what if it wasn't? I turned to race back down the steps when Roger grabbed my arm.

"Should we split up?" he asked, as if we were playing hide-and-go-seek.

"Um ...," I said.

"We should stay together," Gillian said. Her dark curls kinked in a frenzy of excitement. "That way, we can compare notes later."

"Yeah," I said, weak at the knees. "We should stay together."

The main landing of the south tower crested the center front of the castle. It held a huge arched window that boasted a lovely view over the broad drive that ran up to the front steps. In the daylight, when royal guests were expected, a Messenger Boy would wait there to be the first to spot their arrival. Whereupon he would race down to the main level to alert the Footmen.

In the dark, the same window was a black hulk lurking over us. Roger had brought a small lantern from the stables, and now he stopped to light it. Gillian and I waited in the dark. She'd thought to bring one of the paddles that the Laundresses used to ladle clothes into scalding vats. All I'd brought was my wits.

Overhead, a beam creaked. Wind whistled through cracks.

I wrapped my arms around myself. I wished I'd thought to bring a paddle or a candle or maybe even a Guard or two along.

"C-cold?" Gillian asked, teeth chattering.

"Yeah."

"Course it's cold," Roger said, striking a match. "Ain't no fires lit up here."

The match flared. Roger pushed it into the lantern, and the wick caught. A rosy glow filled the space, brightening Roger's face and highlighting Gillian's curls. And silhouetting the head of a beast skulking outside the window.

"Yikes!" I hollered, jumping back.

Gillian spun around, brandishing her paddle. Roger laughed so hard that the lantern bobbed in his grasp, sending splashes of light everywhere.

"Y-you g-guys," he chortled. "It's one of the stone gryphons. It c-can't hurt you!"

"It could," I grumbled under my breath. If I released it with the magic word, that is. I'd done it before. And watching Roger nearly collapse with hilarity tempted me to do it again.

"It's okay." Gillian patted my arm. "It would have startled anyone."

"Let's go look for the ghost," Roger said with a snicker. "Now that you've warned it that we're coming, maybe it will be waiting at the top of the steps to meet us."

"Oh, I hope so!" Gillian said.

"Yeah, me too," I mumbled.

Roger took the lead, lighting the way. The stones at our sides were polished smooth and decorated with carved vines that snaked their way up into the darkness. Our boots echoed on the slate steps; we sounded more like a battalion than three kids. *Boom-boom-boom.* I hoped the ghost was listening and reconsidering its evening adventures.

"So, Roger," Gillian began, "how're we catching this thing?"

"We'll find it first and see what kind of ghost we're dealing with. Then we'll set a trap."

"A trap?" The stone rail felt icy under my hand as I groped my way up the stair. "What kind of a trap?"

"Well, it depends on what kind of a ghost."

Sure. That sounded reasonable.

"You mean like a rabbit trap, where you bait it with a carrot?" Gillian said, obviously warmer to this plan than I was.

"Yeah, sort of."

"What bait?" I said.

"Whatever bait appeals to this kind of ghost," he replied, sounding annoyed.

Clearly, this was all obvious stuff that everybody knew. Everybody but me.

"Jewels might work for this one," Gillian suggested.

"Where are you going to get those?" I snorted. "They don't keep them in the kitchen."

Gillian turned around, a hand on her hip. "You borrow a few from someone who has them."

"The Baroness is rich; she's got lots of jewels," Roger put in. "And you know her, Darling."

"Huh." I could see it now. Me waltzing up to the Baroness to borrow a few jewels to bait my ghost-catching trap.

"We'd give them right back," Gillian explained.

"We have to find the ghost first," I said, crossing my fingers behind my back.

They nodded and started back up the stair. I dragged along behind. When I'd followed the ghost, I'd kept my eye on it. Now it could be anywhere. A prickly sensation

173

tingled between my shoulder blades: what if the ghost snuck up behind me? I darted a glance back—pitch blackness haunted my footsteps. I hurried to catch up to Roger and Gillian.

We scoured the south tower—every room, every nook, every cobweb-laden niche. Our footsteps echoed through the passageways. My fingers cramped with cold. With each draft, I thought of Roger's theory that the chill meant a ghost had passed by. I scrunched my head into my shoulders, anticipating an attack from behind. We saw old trunks, benches, and the occasional wooden chair. But no ghosts. When we reached the top of the tower, we stopped to discuss what to do next.

"We should go back," I suggested, rubbing my aching neck. "Before anybody misses us."

"We could feel for cold spots," Roger offered.

"I'm too frozen to feel anything," Gillian said.

"Should have worn a shawl, then."

"I don't own a shawl."

"Darling has a coat; you could have worn that."

"How would that look?" Gillian said. "Running around *inside* the castle, wearing a coat?"

"Well, you're the one griping about being cold. I'm helping Darling catch this ghost!" Roger shot back.

Not waiting to hear the outcome of this discussion,

I stomped back down the stair. It wound around and around. I felt my way in the dark. My hand brushed a damp, spongy patch on the wall.

"Oh!" I squeaked.

"Hear that?" Roger said, coming down behind me.

The lantern lit the wall, exposing the dampness as mold. Cringing in disgust, I wiped my damp hand on my apron.

"Sounded like a bat," he added.

My scalp threatened to crawl right off my head. I clamped my hands over my hair. It might be fluffy and pale, but it didn't need any bats nesting in it.

"Do you think there's any up here?" Gillian asked, joining us.

"Yeah. You hear it?"

"No," Gillian said. "But I thought I heard a mouse."

"You hear anything, Darling?" he asked.

I shook my head. I was not about to admit that I'd yelped over some mold.

"It doesn't matter," Gillian said. "We're not looking for bats anyway."

"No," Roger said, turning and spilling lantern light all over the stairway. "But I thought I heard one."

"Come on," I said, and hurried down the last of the steps to the main landing.

Once we got there, Roger began prowling around and wandered into the room beyond. Gillian and I trailed after him.

"We've looked here," I said.

"Just making sure," he said, stopping by the far wall.

"Well, maybe we should call it quits for tonight," Gillian said, stifling a yawn. "Your ghost isn't very friendly, Darling. You'd think it would come out to say hi, seeing as how we've given up our evening to look for it."

"*Her* ghost?" Roger said. "I saw it before she did."

"You said you saw it at the same time," Gillian said.

I rolled my eyes.

"Let's—" I froze.

There, smeared on the dusty floor, lit by Roger's lantern, were several footprints. Just lying there on the ground. *They hadn't been there earlier.*

I traced their path with my eye. One, two, three: they led straight into a blank wall—and stopped. The heel of the fourth footprint poked out of the wall, as if the wall had bitten it off.

Or as if the half footprint belonged to a ghost that had walked through the wall. A tremor shook my left leg. Was the ghost still there on the other side of the wall, waiting? *Right this very minute?*

Roger and Gillian argued on, oblivious to what lay on the floor. Any minute now, the ghost could walk back out of the wall. A fit of shivers shook me like a Sweeper beating a rug. Any minute now the ghost could reach out and—

"We have to go back," I said, grabbing Roger by the arm. "Right now."

They looked at me and then at each other.

"She's kinda turned blue," Roger said to Gillian. "Do you think she's cold?"

"Either that or she's seen the ghost," Gillian said.

"Did you?" Roger asked.

I shook my head fiercely. And then, without waiting for them, I took off, putting as much distance between me and that wall as possible.

20

I perched on my stool, hemming a handkerchief with nearly invisible stitches, just the way Marci had shown me. Before becoming Darling the Mending Slave, I'd never held a needle. But I was getting good at sewing. Marci had even started teaching me tricks she used to make the Princess's damaged clothes look like new.

She had given me a little satin box filled with a pincushion, a packet of needles, a pair of scissors, and a ball of beeswax—all for my own. I was now, I reckoned, Darling, Junior Seamstress to Her Majesty. Not that I had an actual job. I was still Marci's charge, pinned to my stool by her occasional sharp glance.

Selma strode in, scrubbing her hands nervously against her sides.

"Good afternoon, Selma," Marci said, scribbling a note in one of the white leather-covered logbooks. "May I help you?"

Selma pursed her lips and dug in her pocket, producing a silver thimble on the tip of her forefinger. She held it up expectantly.

"You found my thimble!" Marci exclaimed, holding out her hand. "Thank you."

"I did." Selma rapped the desk with her thimble-coated finger. "And where do you suppose I found it?"

"I can't imagine," Marci replied, dropping her hand.

"In the laundry room," Selma announced.

"How did it get down there?" Marci asked.

"I thought you might tell me. One of my girls found it in the sawdust."

I felt a funny stirring in the pit of my stomach. The distinct memory of something solid bouncing off the toe of my boot surfaced. I'd felt it the day I found the saltshaker, but I hadn't stopped to investigate.

"Somebody's been playing around in my laundry— moving things, making messes, soiling clean clothes, *stealing*. A saltshaker turned up; I thought a Kitchen Maid was behind the mischief. I had a talking-to with the Head Cook. No, ma'am, none of her girls could be so naughty." Selma blinked back tears. "Then I found this."

Marci stared at her in dismay.

"You can't think *I'd* be behind such things! Not after all the years you've known me!"

"Goodness me, no, Marci! Not you, *her*!" Selma pointed at the pressing room door.

"Lindy?" Marci gasped.

I nearly fell off my stool. Selma was wrong!

"It's not like she and me are friends," Selma said. "Got a temper, that one. Flounces around in that cloak, mooning after the Captain of the Guards. Thinks she's one better than us Under-servants."

"None of that proves guilt," Marci said. "In fact, I can't imagine that Lindy has time to cause trouble. She's either working or with the good Captain."

"It can't be Lindy," I exclaimed. "She'd never spoil someone's hard work. Never."

Selma eyed me. "Then maybe it was you. You turned up that saltshaker."

"It was lying there in the sawdust. I *stepped* on it." I jumped off my stool and faced Selma. "Anybody could have picked up that thimble, put it in a pocket, and lost it. Anybody."

Including you, I wanted to add. But the gleam in Selma's eye stopped me.

She and Lindy had never gotten along. I'd heard Lindy belittle Selma's work time and again. Would she stoop to such deeds? Moving things around . . . maybe. She could have been looking for something. The messes could have been accidents nobody wanted to own up to. Soiled clothes? Maybe they hadn't been clean to start with. But stealing?

I shook the thought loose. Lindy wasn't a thief.

Then I remembered Lady Marguerite's riding skirt. Had it been found? I opened my mouth to ask. But the words died on my tongue. If I admitted that I knew about the skirt, Selma would think I had something to do with it. *Drat.* I'd been Nina at the time. There was no way that I, Darling, Innocent Mender of Hankies, could know anything about that skirt.

I shut my mouth.

"Hmmm," Selma said. "Well, from now on, the Laundresses will be on watch round the clock. Paddles in hand." She slapped the thimble down on the edge of the desk. "We'll see who's behind this. And when I catch 'em— they'll be sorry!"

I wiggled uncomfortably on the cot in Marci's room, where I'd been banished from the Girls' dormitory. Gillian slept in my old bed. That didn't bother me so much when I considered that Francesca was stuck in *her* mother's room. Marci had given me a corner and hung a patterned scarf up like a curtain to give me the illusion of having my own spot.

Marci had a cozy room, one she'd taken a lot of care to decorate with pictures and knickknacks. She gave me a couple of hooks for my clothes and let me keep my wooden crate under my cot. It didn't contain anything but my un-rolled lavender socks. I'd laid them out in the hope that Iago and his family would come and make them their new home. If I ever saw the mice again.

The hooks held my Princess's Girl's uniform and my coat. Mrs. Pepperwhistle had let me keep them—once Marci pointed out that I had no other clothes. Now I knew how the lady in the ghost story felt; she'd had nice clothes, a home, and everything—until she'd lost it all.

I squirmed deeper into my covers. I hadn't said any-thing about the footprints. I wasn't going back to the south tower *ever* if I could help it. Not that we'd had an-other chance to go ghosting, but still, the thought of them made me queasy. I felt safe in Marci's room, high in the east wing. And if anything or anyone could scare a ghost, Marci could.

But I couldn't dismiss the nagging thought that I, Dar-ling the Last Wray, ought to *do* something. I'd seen the ghost around the Princess's room; it could have been in the wardrobe hall. It could have taken the thimble. Some-one had. I just didn't believe it was Lindy.

Marci had forbidden me to warn her. She'd said that would stir up trouble. And we already had plenty of that.

Marci thought a Duster or a Messenger Boy was the likely culprit. If we waited—Selma would catch them and the whole matter would be laid to rest.

I hoped so. I hadn't liked the look she'd given me.

Through the hanging scarf, I heard Marci mumble in her sleep. She wasn't the quietest sleeper in the castle. But even so, I heard a faint shuffling sound coming from the foot of my cot. I clenched my covers, ready to scream. The shuffle became a patter and then a *whump* as something bounded up on my stomach.

Iago, whiskers quivering, stared at me in amazement. Then he dived for my chin and planted a big mousy kiss on it.

"Hey," I said. "Were you worried?"

He leaped back and spread his paws wide as if to say, *How could I not be?*

"But you found me!"

He wrapped his tail around himself and put on his thinking face.

"What is it?"

He crept across my covers. Then he caught a fold of the blanket and pulled it back. At that, he jumped back as if startled, throwing his paw over his heart.

I thought for a moment.

"You found someone else in my bed?"

His whiskers twitched.

"That's Gillian," I whispered. "That's her bed now."

Iago shook his head so hard that his whole body trembled. He balled his little paws and bounced around, punching the air.

"No, don't fight her. It's not her fault." I propped my head on my palm. "Iago, can I ask you for a favor?"

He stood at attention, tail straight up.

"Could you keep an eye on the laundry? And let me know if you see anything suspicious?"

He nodded.

"Thanks," I said. "But be careful. Those Laundresses mean business."

Marci snorted in her sleep; Iago froze. Then, with a flick of his tail, he vanished under the cot.

The kitchen buzzed with the news that the Laundresses guarded the under-cellar, paddles in hand. Selma even stationed one at the bottom of the stairs to demand an accounting from passersby. Not that there were many visitors down there. But still, you'd better have a reason for being there or you weren't welcome.

I took the hint and stayed away.

I had a ghost to catch. But first, I wanted to know what it was doing outside the Princess's door that night. It had taken the pin from the Princess's bedside table and then put it in Francesca's boot. So why did it go back? Was there something about the Princess's room that interested the ghost?

There was only one way to find out.

I bided my time, stitching away. I, Darling, Model Servant, said, *Yes, ma'am* and *No, ma'am* and *Whatever you say, ma'am.* Marci rolled her eyes. I knew she wasn't fooled, but she didn't complain either. I kept working until the waiting baskets disappeared, replaced by piles of neatly mended clothes.

"We'll see what else there is for you to do," Marci said, and gave me a box of buttons. "Meanwhile, sort these."

I stirred the buttons with a finger; a jumble of sizes and colors tumbled over my hand.

"I have important business with the Head Seamstress," Marci said. "Don't forget to check on the canary while I'm gone."

"Oh-kay," I said, unsure how to respond.

She smoothed her hair and straightened her scarf. "I hope someone figures out who played that nasty trick on Francesca, don't you?"

"Sure," I said. "I hope so."

Then Marci *winked* at me and left. I sat, toying with buttons, and wondered if I'd dreamed what I thought I saw. But only for a moment. I dashed to the closet. If Marci wanted me to go, then a-looking I would go.

"I'm back!" I told the dresses.

Lyric chirped, and the whole closet fell into disorder. Hangers clanged. Dresses bounced. Ribbons flew. I laughed out loud. I felt a new, deeper connection to the dresses, which danced with the magic of the Wrays.

"Who wants to go with me?"

Eighty-Two fluttered its multiple layers of scarlet and orange scarves at me. The dress resembled a twist of flames. I slipped into it. Like a lit match, it flared around me, smoldering down to my size.

"You're so beautiful, Eighty-Two," I told it.

But when I turned to the mirror, Selma's reflection confronted me, looking severe.

"Um," I said, struggling to be tactful, "I probably need to be someone else."

Eighty-Two slithered off me into a dejected pool of bright fabric on the floor. I scooped it up and put it back. "I'm sorry."

I picked up Forty-Eight, a deep forest-green velvet embroidered with holly and crimson berries. It had a laced bodice and long pointed sleeves. I stepped into the dress and pulled it up. The laces crimped my waist, and the dress shrank to my size.

But the reflection in the mirror was another Laundress.

"I like *all* the Laundresses," I said hastily as the dresses rustled on their hangers, "but they don't want anyone lurking around their laundry right now."

Lyric banged the side of his cage. I glanced at him. He cocked his head and whistled sharply.

I put the dress back and chose another. Fifty was a marvel of silver lace. I pounced on it before Lyric could object. But once again, the mirror revealed a Laundress.

"No," I said. "I need someone *up here.*"

The dresses stiffened sullenly. Lyric ruffled his feathers and eyed me crossly.

"Please," I added. "I have to go to the Princess's rooms. It's important."

The diamonds on Thirty-Six's shoulder twinkled at me. I picked up the royal-blue silk dress with its dark blue velvet bodice and pinched waist. An elaborate gown, just the sort I imagined the Princess wearing to a ball.

"Perfect," I said, hugging it to me. It hugged me back, scooping me into its soft folds. I whirled around, letting the skirt flare. And then out of the corner of my eye, I caught my reflection.

Mrs. Pepperwhistle stood in the mirror, twirling her skirt.

21

I stumbled midtwirl and landed in a heap on the floor. Mrs. Pepperwhistle eyed me from the floor of the mirror. I untangled my feet from Thirty-Six's skirt. She untangled hers. It was unnerving. I stood up and dusted Thirty-Six off.

Lyric chirped at me. One Hundred folded its lace sleeves across its bodice. The other dresses twisted on their hangers. If they'd had feet, they'd have tapped their toes.

Well, I'd asked for someone who could be in the upper-regions. And Mrs. Pepperwhistle could go anywhere.

"It's, um, perfect," I said.

Thirty-Six squeezed me in appreciation. Lyric shook out his tail feathers. I had the distinct impression that he wasn't fooled. But I waved to the closet.

"Thanks so much!" I said as I ducked out the door.

I scooted through the wardrobe hall. Marci and Lindy were gone, and Gillian didn't dare stick her nose out of the pressing room for fear of being sent back downstairs. She loved working upstairs—as much as she loved stories, and *that* was saying something. I strolled straight to the corridor by the Princess's rooms. I wanted another look at that wall.

The corridor was deserted this time of day. The Laundresses had come and gone earlier. The Princess herself was off doing whatever princesses do. And the Princess's Girls would already have tidied up by now. I strolled past the closed-up King's Suite to the end of the corridor, running my hands over the wall's spotless surface. No spooky chill. Nothing. No hint that any ghost had passed this way. I crouched down and studied the floor. No sign of footprints. The Maids had obliterated any trace the ghost might have left.

Frustrated, I pushed my palm against the wall, closing my eyes and holding my breath. Magic trickled under my hand like a slow-moving stream. I didn't want to dabble too deeply in it; I didn't want to rouse the dragons. But I needed a *touch*, a spoonful of magic. Just enough to lift my spirit.

Magic bubbled against my palm, soothing away worry and fear. The magic wasn't afraid of the dragons, and it certainly wasn't afraid of any moldy old ghost.

"You're only a troublemaker," I said loudly enough for the ghost to hear. "You're no match for me and the castle. You'll see."

And then I released the wall and stalked out of the dormitory and straight down to the Princess's rooms. I held my head high and my skirt close. I, Darling Pepperwhistle, was mistress of all things domestic. I swept down the corridor to the large double doors leading into the Princess's suite.

I stopped a moment to admire them. Tall, broad, measured into six panels each, trimmed with gold, and meeting in the middle in a large gold crest. The doors leading into the wardrobe hall had gold trim and a crest, but these doors were decorated with painted landscapes. I gawped at them. The gold trim floated over a scene from fairyland—flowers, trees, ponds, and fountains—glistening with gold dust. It was like looking through a window into another, forbidden world.

I twisted my hands together. I'd almost *pounded* on this door! I snuck a glance over my shoulder. No one stood behind me. No one was watching. Steeling myself, I reached out and turned the gold knob. The door floated open.

I stepped through into the Princess's anteroom, an entryway painted to resemble a flowering meadow with a flock of butterflies flitting about and fleecy clouds overhead. Three doors broke the walls. I guessed that the center door led straight to Her Highness's bedroom, so I opened it.

A darkened room greeted me. The curtains were closed, which was unusual. I squinted at the canopied bed, making sure no one was in it. I stepped inside and let my eyes adjust to the dimness. In the gloom, it appeared that snow lay scattered over the carpet. A snow that glinted here and there almost metallically.

Snow?

I stepped forward, expecting my boot to squish the snow and sink into nothingness. I bent down and touched the fluffy whiteness. Feathers. The floor was covered with feathers.

Then I noticed that the mound of pillows was missing from the bed. The coverlet had been pulled aside, and the blanket had been tossed in a mangled pile. I'd never seen such careless housekeeping! If I really were Pepperwhistle, I'd be furious. Those Princess's Girls would all be fired.

I couldn't linger. I needed to hurry. The carved headboard panels huddled in the dark. I touched them. They felt normal, solid. Safe. No chill, no evidence of the ghost's presence.

Then I heard it—a muffled mumbling, as if someone was whispering over and over, *Six and seven, six and seven.*

It was an eerie, breathless whisper, as though it flowed from airless lungs. Gooseflesh covered my arms. The back of my neck prickled.

The ghost mumbled on, unaware that I was listening. It was there somewhere. I didn't see it. But it was there.

Clutching Thirty-Six close, I headed back toward the door. My foot crunched something on the floor. I lifted my skirt and peered down. The remains of a pearl lay beneath my shoe. Pieces of the Princess's jewelry glinted at me from under the feathers. My mouth dried up.

I'd crushed the clasp of one of her bracelets. I felt faint. Looking around, I saw what I should have noticed right away—open drawers and cabinet doors.

The ghost had ransacked the Princess's bedroom! I gasped in horror.

And any moment now, someone could walk in and discover it. *And me*, disguised as Mrs. Pepperwhistle. What would I say then?

My heart pounded. I had to get out of there. Kicking feathers aside, I fled.

22

The news shook the castle like a violent storm. Captain Bryce set Guards at the Princess's suite and the entrance to the wardrobe hall. Mrs. Pepperwhistle ordered those under her to work in pairs. No one was to go anywhere alone. Under-servants were told to stay below. Marsdon, the Head Steward, took to patrolling the halls.

Upper-servants and Under-servants watched each other with squinty-eyed stares. The atmosphere between them iced over with a frosty distrust. Since I was industriously sorting buttons when the real Mrs. Pepperwhistle discovered the disaster in the Princess's room, and Gillian was bent over her ironing in the pressing room, neither of us was under any particular suspicion. At least, not any more than I'd been under to begin with. The Head Cook announced to anyone who'd listen that while Darling had her faults (fortunately, she neglected to list them), she was not a wanton destroyer of beautiful things.

It was a good thing she didn't know about the pearl bracelet, or she might have thought differently. As it was, Marci kept an even closer eye on me than before. Only now it seemed as though she was standing guard over me, not so much to keep me out of trouble as to be able to vouch for my whereabouts. There was a certain comfort in knowing Marci stood between me and any pointing fingers.

Selma made a show of overseeing deliveries to the wardrobe hall. When the Laundresses marched in, hefting their heavy baskets of linens, Selma was there with a piercing gaze and a freshly cleaned gown in her red-knuckled grip. She made a ceremony of handing clothes over to Lindy, who took them with an equal air of solemnity. The two reminded me of a pair of Guardsmen changing posts.

I was surprised that Selma didn't lug her paddle around with her. As it was, she made a point of taking a quick tour around the wardrobe hall, as if the intruder was concealed there unbeknownst to the rest of us. Marci expressed her irritation by banging the closet doors as she fetched Her Highness's things.

Tempers were frayed on every level. Even Lady Kaye,

armed with her silver-topped cane, took it upon herself to stand by the Princess at all times. You had to pity anyone foolish enough to mess with Princess Mariposa while the Baroness was at hand.

I was just picturing the Baroness dispatching the thief when a shadow fell over my sewing.

"What are you doing?" Lady Kaye inquired.

"Setting a sleeve," I said.

The lustrous pile of violet silk jacquard before me almost melted at the touch. It took care and patience to sew the tiny stitches reattaching the sleeve to the bodice. Marci had done the tricky stuff; she'd altered the shape of the sleeve before handing it to me to reset. She'd rounded up several dresses she thought needed restyling—they probably didn't, but the work kept me busy.

"That is very expensive fabric," Lady Kaye remarked.

"Darling does excellent work," Marci told her, snipping a thread on a hem. "Otherwise I wouldn't allow her to handle the Princess's clothes."

"I thought she was Lindy's assistant," Lady Kaye said, tapping her cane on the carpet.

"She was, once upon a time," Marci answered, and selected a new spool of thread from one of the desk drawers.

Lady Kaye frowned, glancing around the wardrobe hall.

"Are those closets kept locked?" she asked.

"They are," Marci replied, "except for the old Queen's closet. The key's been misplaced."

"Since when?" Lady Kaye demanded.

"Since before I was Wardrobe Mistress," Marci said.

Lady Kaye glowered at the door to Queen Candace's closet as if it had deliberately left itself unlocked.

"We'll have to see about that," she said.

The stool rocked beneath me as I swayed in my seat.

"I'll have the Royal Locksmith cast a new key," Lady Kaye said.

She wouldn't! Would she?

I caught Marci's eye. *Don't let her lock it up,* I pleaded silently.

"Not to worry," Marci said. "That key is likely around here somewhere."

Guards opened the wardrobe hall door as Footmen carried in three bolts of cloth.

"Right here by the desk, please," Marci said, rising. "You can lay them on the carpet."

The Footmen laid the three bolts down and left. A Guard winked at me as he shut the door. Marci walked over to the dressing room and cracked open the door.

"The fabric is here, Your Highness," she said.

Princess Mariposa appeared, wearing a severe charcoal-colored dress. She had taken to wearing darker dresses since her room had been torn apart, as if her clothes reflected the seriousness of the crimes committed against her. I hadn't seen her in days; she walked past me without a glance.

"Oh dear, however will I decide?" she said.

She unrolled each of the bolts—royal-blue velvet, sapphire brocade glistening with gold threads, and a sky-blue satin woven all over with silver.

"Simple, my dear," Lady Kaye exclaimed. "Keep them all. The velvet for afternoons, the brocade for court, and the satin for a ball." She pointed her cane at each one as she spoke.

"Ball!" The Princess's voice rang through the room. "I'm not hosting any ball."

"You should," Lady Kaye said. "There's enough gloom in winter without adding to it."

Princess Mariposa sighed. Behind her, the pressing room door opened. Lindy and Gillian sidled in. No doubt they'd been listening at the door, and the mention of a ball was too irresistible to ignore.

"Oh, but you'd look a picture in that satin, Your Highness," Lindy said.

"Think how it would cheer up the court to see you dancing again," Marci offered.

"I've heard the Prince is partial to blue," Gillian added.

"This sounds like a conspiracy." Princess Mariposa favored them with a wry smile.

"Oh no, ma'am, we haven't been conspiring!" Gillian said, face flushed.

Lady Kaye took in Gillian's brown dress and canvas apron and shook her head.

"Shouldn't that girl wear the proper attire of her station?" she asked.

"She should," the Princess said. "It's not like Francesca to be so lax." She colored as she realized what she'd said. "Lindy, tell—Ann—isn't it? Tell Ann to find her some clothes."

Gillian beamed at the notion of wearing the gray dresses and crisp white aprons. I'd never seen her so pleased. Her expression made me smile too.

"Thank you, Your Highness!" she said.

The Princess nodded absently and said, "Marci, order all three dresses. Tell the seamstress I'd like the velvet finished first. The ball gown can be last." She eyed the Baroness. "Not that I'll need it."

"You might surprise yourself, dear," Lady Kaye said.

"I already have," Princess Mariposa said. She caught my smile and held my eye with a measuring gaze.

I thought she would finally speak to me again, but disappointment etched her brow and she turned away. Gripping my needle in despair, I watched her leave. I wanted to shout after her, *I didn't steal anything!* But I went back to work with a sigh.

"In my day, we threw a proper number of balls," Lady Kaye said.

"Oh," Gillian said, dimples deepening. "Were they very fancy?"

"I should say so," Lady Kaye replied.

"You'd probably like to hear all about 'em," Lindy said, poking Gillian in the shoulder. "This one likes stories."

"I know any number of stories," Lady Kaye said, caressing the knob of her cane. "If you're finished with your work, you can rub my feet while I tell them to you."

I winced at the thought of the Baroness's feet.

"I'm done, aren't I?" Gillian asked Lindy.

"Get off with you," Lindy said, shooing her. "I have a pack of things to do."

"And Captains to meet," Marci said under her breath.

Needle drooping, I watched as they left. Gillian was a real Princess's Girl, and I was . . . I wasn't sure what I was anymore.

23

"Those Guards are a problem," Roger said, sprinkling his soup with salt. "You can forget going into the Princess's rooms with them around."

We'd met early for supper so that we could plot our next ghosting without being overheard—and without Gillian. She'd stuck to my heels since getting her new clothes, walking with a bounce in her step. Patting the embroidered butterfly on her apron pocket as if she needed to reassure herself it was still there. She'd even been given a bright blue ribbon she threaded through her curls and tied in a bow. One of the Guards had started calling her *little lady.*

Not that she was any better than the rest of us.

And worst of all, the Baroness had taken to sending for

Gillian in the late afternoon. According to her, the Baroness knew more stories than everyone else who'd ever lived. I doubted that, but I was smart enough not to say so.

"But we need a dress. How're we going to search the castle without one?" I asked.

"The Guards are there all the time. Say you walk into the wardrobe hall and then get a dress—someone different would walk back out," Roger replied, dipping a piece of bread into his soup. "That's bound to raise questions."

"I could go back out through the Princess's room."

"There're Guards there too," he said, shaking his head.

"But they're different guards."

"So you walk in and Lady—*Redhead*—walks out the other door, but then *you* never come back out. Pretty soon, someone's going to wonder what became of Darling and go looking. When they realize you're not there, they'll ask the other Guards."

"But Lady Redhead will come back—"

"Okay, say she does. How're you going to explain where *you* were that whole time?"

Exasperated, I stirred my bowl of soup so hard it sloshed over the rim.

"Just forget it," Roger said. "We'll think of something else."

"You could cause a distraction," I argued. "Then I could duck in, grab a dress, and go."

Roger considered that for a moment. "How am I going to distract both of them without getting in trouble? I don't have any business bein' up there."

"Um." I stuck a spoonful of soup in my mouth to buy myself time to think.

"Once again, you'd have to go back. And *whoever* you'd walked in as wouldn't walk back out. Sooner or later, they'd notice."

"We're never going to get this ghost."

"Sure we are. We're just not going to use the dresses."

"How? Everybody is watching everybody."

"I'll think of something," Roger said.

His smile flattened into a determined line, and his brow contracted. You could see his brain churning, one idea tumbling over another. He had the same look the Footmen got when they polished the silver. Then his face cleared.

"Almost forgot to tell you," he said, brightening. "I got put in charge of a horse."

"Does the horse know where the ghost is?" I tore off a piece of bread. Then it hit me. "Hey, I thought Second Stable Boys didn't get horses!"

He grinned so widely his freckles almost popped off his cheeks.

"The Stable Master pulled me aside and said, *Here, you're in charge of Lady Marguerite's horse. Let's see how you do*," he said.

"Lady Marguerite's horse!" I leaned over my soup bowl. "What a coincidence."

"Seems that way," he said, smirking. "But a First Stable Boy said he'd overheard Pepperwhistle talking to the Stable Master—Lady Marguerite thinks I've got talent."

"Huh." I'd accidentally gotten Roger a chance at a promotion.

"I'll be a First Stable Boy before you know it." Roger beamed, tweaking his forelock. Obviously, he was already picturing himself in the buff-colored leather cap the First Boys wore.

"That's great, Roger," I said. Then I did a mock bow in my seat. "You're welcome."

He laughed so hard that several heads turned our way.

I tucked into my bread. I was happy for him. Really. But any day now he'd be a First Stable Boy and Gillian would be a Princess's Girl and I'd be ... Darling Unfortunate, Mending Nobody. It didn't seem fair.

The kitchens began to fill up with servants wandering in for their supper. The Head Cook roamed about, sampling sauces, testing a roast goose with a fork, and generally keeping an eye on her troops. Supper for the servants was already set out and waiting; now the real work began—dinner for Her Highness. The Head Cook prided herself on serving a perfect meal on time every evening. The staff chopped, stirred, roasted, and sautéed like mad;

they would rather be cooked with the goose than serve Her Highness something less than excellent.

I was ready to suggest that we finish up and go see the horse when Roger's eyes brightened. He was about to speak when a pair of mittens landed on the table next to me.

"I thought you might be needing these," Jane said, standing over me.

"Good evening, Jane," I said, wondering what kind of mood she was in.

I'd been avoiding her. Losing the Princess's trust made me feel terrible, but disappointing Jane had been even worse. If not for Jane, I wouldn't be in the castle at all. She'd been broken up over my losing my position. But this latest mess ... if she thought I'd had anything to do with it, she'd be livid.

"Try them on," Jane said, sitting down beside me and giving me a blurry-eyed grin.

The mittens were a soft silver color, knit from kitten-soft yarn, with pewter-buttoned velvet cuffs, edged with silver cord. I picked them up.

"They're beautiful." I unbuttoned the cuffs to discover an inside layer of rose pink. I slid the mittens on. "They're so soft!"

Roger rolled his eyes. He wore heavy suede gloves to work outside. They were stained from cleaning up after horses, which were way too messy, in my opinion.

"I worked a little swan's down into the lining," Jane explained. "That'll make them warmer too."

"Thank you!" I threw my arms around her.

She hugged me back, and then she whispered in my ear, "What's this business about the Princess's room?"

I tensed up.

"Darling?" she said, pulling away.

"I had nothing to do with that!" I said. "I would never do such a thing."

She squinted, studying me as best she could. "I didn't think so. My Darling is not vicious; that's what I told the Head Steward."

She let me go and sat back.

The Head Steward had been asking about me? I didn't like the sound of that.

"Marci swears you never went in there," she continued. "I hear it was terrible, spiteful. The rat who done it even ground one of Her Highness's pearls to powder!"

The room swam. I'd scoured the bottom of my boot to remove any trace of pearl dust. But what if I'd left some along the way? What if there was a pearly trail leading right to me? No one would ever believe that I'd walked in the room *after* it had been ransacked. Not that I had any reason for being in there in the first place.

"Well—" I said.

"What have you got there?" the Head Cook asked.

I jumped in my seat, startled, certain that incriminating pearl dust still clung to me.

"I made her mittens," Jane said. "Show her, Darling."

Smothering a sigh, I pulled them off and handed them to the Head Cook.

"Oh my, my," she said. "You made these, Jane? They are lovely."

"I knit them; Marci sewed the cuffs."

"Where did you get the materials—velvet and pewter, no less?"

"Marci got the fabric and the buttons from the Head Seamstress. I had one of the Under-dusters get me the wool; her father has a shop in the city."

"Could you make me a pair? I'd be happy to pay for them."

Jane started. "Sure. What color?"

"A nice brown with fur cuffs!"

"Fur cuffs?" Jane squeaked.

"I'll supply the fur," the Head Cook said, handing the mittens back to me. "And what about a hood to match, could you knit one of those?"

"I can."

"I'll get the fur and the yarn," the Head Cook said, licking her lips as if she could already taste her new mittens. And she stalked off as though she meant to get the materials right then.

"If Marci doesn't want to sew on the cuffs, I could help," I said.

"Thank you, dear." Jane patted my arm. Then she added in a whisper, "Stay in the kitchens, where everyone can see you. The Head Steward has his spies watching."

Her blurry blue gaze cleared momentarily as if she could see right through me. Her mouth crimped at the corner. A feisty hardness gripped her jaw. She had the look of a Laundress about to wring out a petticoat.

"Don't get in trouble for my sake," I said.

"Don't be silly," she said, getting up. "I have to go talk to Agnes."

She left, feeling her way as she went.

"Jane's nice," Roger said, finishing his soup. "But I wouldn't want to be her enemy."

"Me neither," I said, trying to imagine Jane having enemies.

24

That night I set out a piece of my leftover bread. No sooner had Marci begun mumbling in her sleep than Iago appeared at the foot of my cot, whiskers wiggling as he nibbled the edges of the bread.

"How are things in the laundry?" I asked.

He held up his paw to signal that he wasn't finished with his snack. I waited patiently until he patted his belly.

"Did you find out who's bothering the Laundresses?"

His eyes darted from side to side.

"You looked everywhere?"

He nodded, then slid a fold of blanket over his head and sank down so that only his eyes were visible.

"You hid and watched."

He popped up and threw his paws wide, holding only empty air.

"You didn't find anything." I sank back into my pillow.

He crept over and settled against my shoulder, blinking sadly.

"It's all right," I said. "Thanks for looking."

He sniffed the air but otherwise said nothing.

"You're a huge help, Iago. And a great friend."

His nose twitched.

"Maybe you can check up on the dresses for me?"

His head popped up. His ears quivered.

"You have something to say?"

He stood very still, and then he turned his head to the right, stopped, and then turned his head to the left. He repeated this, and then he took a step.

"Watch where you're going?" I guessed.

He put his paw over his eyes.

"Oh! Watch where *I'm* going? You mean I should watch my step!"

He scurried up to me and tapped me on the nose. His tiny black eyes gleamed with concern.

"Okay," I said. "I will."

He flipped his tail and disappeared into the darkness. I snuggled into my pillow, squeezing it a bit to smooth out the lumps. *Watch my step . . . ,* I thought as sleepiness tugged at me. What steps? Did Iago think I might fall? Or step into more trouble?

What more trouble could I possibly get into?

Gillian traced her iron over a handkerchief, dissolving the wrinkles. She tilted her head to one side, as if listening to faraway music while she worked. She kept one hand tucked into her hip as she swayed to a silent beat.

She existed in her own world, one that included Lindy, the Baroness and her stories, and the Princess, but not me. I chewed my lip as I waited, holding a freshly mended pile of handkerchiefs out to her.

"They're done," I said at last, tired of holding them. Tired of watching her. Tired of being left out.

"Oh!" She started and whipped around, a blazing iron in her fist.

"Watch that," I grumbled. "It's hot."

"Sorry!" she sang, taking the handkerchiefs. "I got lost in my ironing, it's so soothing."

Soothing? Ha!

"Ann told me that Francesca couldn't stand how you were so good at it," she said. "Something about her sister."

"Faustine, that's her name."

"Yes, Faustine and Francesca. They have a younger sister named Faye. She lives with their grandmother."

"How would you know that?"

"Kate told me." Gillian smiled, and her dimples creased. "They talk all the time, those Girls. They never shut up."

I felt steam rising from the iron, which was almost as hot as my face.

"They never talked to me!" I blurted out.

Gillian frowned. "Course not. They thought you took away Faustine's job."

"The Princess fired her. Cherice and Lindy came and got *me*. You were there. I had nothing to do with it!"

"I know," she said, shrugging her shoulders. "Weird, huh?"

My fingers curled into fists.

"So," she said, lowering her voice, "when are we going to go look for that ghost?"

She looked so concerned, so eager, that all my irritation melted away.

"Soon as Roger thinks up a plan."

"Count me in," she said. "Count me *in*."

By evening, I was famished, exhausted, and anxious. Roger had said he was going to come up with a plan. I sped down the corridor on my way to supper. I needed that plan now! Not later. And I intended to tell him so.

Politely, of course.

Ann and Kate rounded the corner, dragging Dulcie between them.

"Stop! Cut it out!" she squalled. Her face was tear-stained, and her braid disheveled. Her apron looked like someone had used it to clean the floor.

I pulled up short. "Hey," I said. "What's going on?"

"We found this one *hiding* in the scullery," Ann said.

"We've been looking for her for hours," Kate added.

"How come? What's she done?"

"Spilled a pitcher all over the dormitory floor. Soaked the rugs! And she's going to clean it up!" Ann added, giving Dulcie a shake.

I dug out my handkerchief.

"Let her go; let her clean off her face. It was an accident."

"How would you know?" Kate said. "You weren't there."

Dulcie sniffled and hiccuped at the same time.

"It—it wasn't me," she wailed.

"There, it wasn't her," I said.

"Likely story," Kate snipped.

"Did you see it happen?" I asked, my temper rising. "Just because there was a mess doesn't mean she made it."

Ann and Kate exchanged a guilty look.

Ann dropped Dulcie's arm. "Okay, clean up."

Dulcie took the handkerchief and dried her eyes. That didn't make her face any cleaner, but she looked relieved.

"What was she doing hiding in the scullery?" Kate demanded.

Dulcie hiccuped again, silently pleading with me. I realized she'd been hiding so she could cry. And I could just imagine what Ann and Kate would make of that.

"She's a little kid; she was probably scared. Right, Dulcie? Those Messenger Boys are mean." I tousled her hair.

"They are," she agreed, nodding solemnly.

"Go get cleaned up. Fast. Or there won't be any supper for you," Ann threatened.

"And don't get any of that filth on the beds," Kate added.

Dulcie nodded and streaked down the hall.

Ann eyed me. "I see you've developed a sympathy for the criminal element in the castle."

"Two peas in a pod," Kate said.

"I'd rather be like Dulcie than you two. Sand-spreading, glue-dumping sneaks," I shot back.

They cringed, shocked into silence. That reminded me; I hadn't told on them. Yet.

Six and seven, six and seven, the ghost moaned. I wandered through the dark corridors, skin prickling, clutching a burned-out candle. The walls rattled at me, clanging like the dresses on their hangers. I looked down. I was wearing one. A greasy, grimy, torn black dress.

"Who are you?" I asked.

The dress slithered around my knees, binding them. The walls leaned closer.

Six and seven, the ghost screamed.

A hand grabbed me. The Head Steward loomed out of the darkness.

"I have you now!" he snarled.

I woke with a start, heart pounding, and sat straight up in bed. Something sharp pierced my arm. I shook it off.

Iago landed with a *thump* on my covers, eyes rolling back in his head.

"I'm sorry," I said, scooping him up. "Are you all right?"

He glared at me as if to say, *Watch where you throw things.*

"I had a bad dream," I explained. "I thought something had a hold of me."

He shook his head.

"That was you, wasn't it? You were trying to wake me up?" I shifted in bed, and something crackled beneath me. I felt under the blanket with my free hand and found a piece of paper. I pulled it out. Iago spread his paws as if to say, *Voilà.*

"You brought this for me?"

His head bobbed.

"Thank you." I squinted at it. It was too dark to see.

"You're the best, Iago. I'll have to find you a nice hunk of cheese."

He dipped his head at the paper as if to say, *And?*

"I can't read it in the dark. Can you tell me what it says?" I asked hopefully.

He spread out his paws and turned in a circle. Then he jumped down out of my palm.

A circle? A ball? Was this about the Princess holding a ball? Or—a sudden bolt of insight struck me—was this about a dress?

"This is about the dresses?" I guessed.

His ears drooped in disappointment.

"I'll have to read it in the morning," I told him.

He scratched his head, flicked his whiskers, and disappeared.

I folded the paper and slid it under my pillow. I lay down, but I had a hard time getting back to sleep. Every time I closed my eyes, I heard the echo of *six and seven* and felt the Head Steward's grasp.

25

"You're going to be late," Marci said, shaking me awake.

I tumbled out of bed. "I'll be right there."

"You'd better be." She smoothed her crown of braids. "You have shoes to polish."

Marci had made good on her promise to keep me occupied. And while the tasks weren't always exciting, they kept me close to the closet. Even if I couldn't figure out how to use a dress.

"Good," I said.

She left and I pulled on my clothes, tying my apron in a well-practiced bow. I dashed a comb through my hair and, as I was about to leave, saw a folded paper on the floor. Iago's note. I snatched it up and stuffed it in my pocket.

Leather shoes of every color and style covered the desk

in the wardrobe hall. Next to them was a tin marked MINK OIL and a pile of clean rags. The dressing room door stood open by a hairbreadth, and the sound of voices floated out. Marci was dressing Princess Mariposa.

I shifted from foot to foot. I'd seen servants polish boots, but I'd never learned how they did it. I picked up a rag and a shoe, a glossy black leather with a spray of diamonds over the toes. I peered inside; the diamonds were part of a clip fastened to the shoe. Should I take them off? Leave them on? Would the polish ruin the diamonds?

I put the shoe back down; I had enough problems in my life. I didn't need any more. I dropped the rag, took a deep breath, and listened. I heard Marci talking to the Princess, and Lindy lecturing Gillian in the pressing room. It was time to feed Lyric; I dived into the closet.

Sun blazed through the stained-glass window. The dresses fluttered. Lyric trilled his delight. Crystals flashed. Flounces stirred. Hangers tinkled merrily.

"Good morning," I told the dresses.

Lyric chirped as I slid the drawer out of the cage and filled it. Then I popped it back in.

"Enjoy," I told him.

A grass-green ribbon wiggled my way. I couldn't wear the dresses anywhere, but I could try one on. Just one. For a minute or two. I started to follow it.

The closet door flew open.

"Ready?" Marci asked, eyeing my outstretched hand.

"Yes, ma'am." I snatched my hand back. "I fed the canary."

"Good." Her lips twitched, but she didn't say anything.

I followed her to the desk to learn the art of shoe polishing. Each shoe had to be rubbed with mink oil (after decorations were removed) and buffed with a cloth. Then lavender-scented sachets were packed into the toes. Marci informed me that the shoes on the desk were only the beginning of a long parade of footwear.

"Wonderful," I said, although I'd rather sew.

"The Head Seamstress is fitting Her Highness's new court dress, so I need to get back in there," she said, leaving me to it.

I polished away until Selma arrived, a petticoat draped over her arm.

"Is Lindy here?" she asked in a clipped tone.

"Yes, ma'am, right in there," I said, pointing at the door.

Marci came out of the dressing room just as I spoke.

"Good morning, Selma," she said.

"It would be if a certain person did her job," Selma retorted.

"Which person are you referring to?" Marci asked, reaching for a pair of blue shoes. "I am currently busy doing mine."

Princess Mariposa called from the doorway, "Marci, not the blue."

She wore a gown of sapphire brocade woven with gold threads. A tiny line creased her forehead. She held her arms up, away from the silver pins tacked into the bodice at her sides. Pins dotted the hem that flared behind her in a long train. The ragged ends of unfinished armholes feathered around her shoulders. More pins marked where sleeves would be added.

"Darling's polished the black with diamonds," Marci answered. "Perhaps you would prefer those?" She picked up the shoes to offer them to the Princess.

"Maybe. What is that?" the Princess asked, gesturing at Selma's arm.

"A petticoat, Your Highness," Selma announced, unfolding the undergarment to reveal a jagged edge around the bottom. "Someone's ripped the lace right off the bottom."

"Is that an old garment?" the Princess asked.

"No, Your Majesty, it's new. I found it in a basket collected from the Head Presser."

The Princess opened the pressing room door.

"Lindy," she said. "Please come here."

Setting her iron down with a bang, Lindy popped out of the pressing room.

"Lindy, explain this," the Princess said, gesturing to the petticoat.

"I—I don't know anything about it!" Lindy gaped at the ruined garment.

"It was in the basket you sent down," Selma retorted.

"I collected those clothes from Marci," Lindy replied.

"That petticoat was intact when I put it in the basket last night," Marci said, clutching the shoes against her chest.

A tiny crease formed in the Princess's forehead.

"Does that basket stay under *her* charge?" Selma said, pointing at Lindy.

"Now, you see here—" Lindy said.

"I wouldn't put it past you to slip something into the bottom of the basket so that *my* gals is blamed for it," Selma interrupted.

"What?" Lindy exploded. "Why would I do that?"

The Princess moved to interrupt, but Selma waved the petticoat under Lindy's nose.

"Malice, pure and simple," Selma said. "I have reason to believe that you've been a-messin' with my laundry!"

"Ladies, ladies!" Marci waved the shoes to get their attention.

"Messing with your laundry?" Lindy turned a dark purple. "I wouldn't step foot there for all the cake in the kingdom!"

"Somebody left a saltshaker and a thimble in my laundry—explain that!" Selma cried.

"Enough!" Princess Mariposa roared, her cheeks crimson.

I rocked in my seat; I'd never seen the Princess so angry before. Marci nearly dropped the shoes. Lindy blanched. Selma took a step back.

The Princess clapped a hand over her mouth. Her brow furrowed. Her whole face burned with embarrassment. Marci, Lindy, and Selma shrank inward like a fallen soufflé. The three eyed one another guiltily.

Princess Mariposa took her hand away from her mouth and drew herself up regally.

"Now then," she continued in a softer tone, "I want to know what is going on around here. Who is tampering with my things?"

"I've seen Selma wearing your white shawl—that one with the tassels!" Lindy announced triumphantly. "Ask her what's going on."

Selma wheeled around as if struck.

"*I* gave that to the Head Laundress for her own use," Princess Mariposa said, her eyes darkening to sapphire. "Am I not free to bestow my things on whomever I wish?"

"I didn't know," Lindy said in a small voice. "My apologies, Selma."

Selma nodded sharply. I realized I'd been rubbing the same shoe for several minutes and set it down.

"I don't know what's going on," Marci said, placing the

blue shoes on the desk before me. "But I assure you, Your Highness, that none of us would abuse your trust."

I cringed. Marci meant well, but when she said it, the others glanced at me. Selma grimaced and Lindy looked pained.

"Very well," Princess Mariposa said. "Selma, hand that to Lindy. Lindy, that's new fabric; find a use for it—repair it, reuse it, do something so that it's not wasted!"

Without another word, Lindy took the petticoat, curtsied, and went back to the pressing room, closing the door silently behind her. Selma, seizing her chance, bobbed her head and left. Marci and I held our breaths to hear what Her Highness would say next.

"We'll get to the bottom of this later," Princess Mariposa told Marci. Then she took a deep breath and smoothed the waist of her unfinished gown.

I caught sight of a woman hiding behind the dressing room door. The Head Seamstress, most likely. From the shocked expression on her face, she had no intention of stepping out into the wardrobe hall. I didn't blame her. I wished I were a thousand miles away.

"The black shoes, Darling, please," the Princess said, her voice unsteady.

I snatched up the shoes and presented them to her.

"I polished them," I said.

The Princess looked at the shoes in my hand and gestured to the floor. I stood there awkwardly. Marci took them from me and helped Her Highness step into them. The Princess turned her foot from side to side under the fabric of her skirt.

"I don't know," she said, biting her lower lip. "All these decisions: ribbons! jewels! shoes! The bother of having new clothes!"

"The Baroness probably thought that some new gowns would cheer you up," I offered in a tiny voice.

That startled Princess Mariposa. She winced as if she felt a bit guilty—and a little chagrined. She looked as though she might cry.

But she was a princess through and through. She steadied herself and took off the shoes.

"Not black," she said with a weak smile. "Something else?"

"Matching shoes covered in the brocade?" Marci suggested.

"Gold dust," I said.

"What?" Princess Mariposa's head came up.

"Maybe you should have gold shoes," the Head Seamstress offered from her hiding spot.

"That might be pretty." Marci tugged at her scarf.

"Gold-dusted blue leather," I said, gathering my nerve.

"They would shine every time you took a step. All-gold shoes would stand out against that dark sapphire. They'd be more noticeable."

The Princess pressed her lips together, considering.

"They'd be pretty, but gold-dusted blue shoes would be subtle. More princesslike, Your Highness . . ." My voice faded under her gaze.

"That's an excellent point," she replied.

"Shoes like those would be unique," Marci said.

"I know the Royal Cobbler would enjoy the challenge," the Head Seamstress said.

"Order them," the Princess said to Marci. And then she turned to me. "Thank you," she said with a smile.

My heart sang. She'd smiled at me!

"I'm really sorry, Your Highness. I only borrowed the book because I wanted to read it. That's all," I said, anxious for her to understand.

A knowing light came into her eyes. "I believe you," she said. "But there *is* something you're not telling me."

My face froze.

"Who did it?" she demanded. "Who took my pin?"

My pulse pounded in my ears. I twisted my hands together. I tried to say that I didn't know, but my lips refused to move. I couldn't lie to her.

"Darling!"

"The ghost did it!" I said with a sob.

There, I'd said it. Now she knew.

The color drained from Princess Mariposa's face. She stiffened. "I thought I meant more to you than that," she said. "I thought I had your respect, the respect due me as your sovereign. I see I was wrong."

She turned on her heel and left, closing the dressing room door behind her.

26

"A ghost?" Marci exclaimed, cuffing me on the head. "Are you daft?"

"But I saw it!" I wailed.

Marci pursed her lips, considering me the way she would an unraveled hem.

"There are no such things as ghosts," she replied.

"But you know there are! There's that old woman in the south tower and—"

"That's just a story," she said.

"You made it up?"

"The story about the old woman's mysterious disappearance is true, but that doesn't mean there are ghosts."

"But the servants heard her. Saw her. How can you say there are no ghosts?"

"They heard *something*. They saw *something*. And they believed what they heard and saw was a ghost because that's what they were expecting." Marci sighed. "I've lived in this castle my whole life and never seen a ghost. I don't believe in them."

"But I did," I whimpered. "The night the pin disappeared, I saw it."

"I'm sure you thought you did," Marci said, patting my arm. "I have to get back to the Princess. Polish the shoes and I'll see what I can say to Her Highness."

Marci tucked a stray lock of hair back into her braids. Steeling herself, she marched back into the dressing room.

A row of shoes waited for me. I picked one up. Marci thought I imagined seeing the ghost. Princess Mariposa thought I was making it up to avoid telling her what I knew. I dipped the rag in the mink oil. My heart felt torn down the middle. I'd told the truth. I shouldn't have, because nobody believed it. But I had.

The truth was the truth; some mean, nasty old ghost was wreaking havoc in the castle. I sat up a little straighter. I, Darling Wray Fortune, Ghost Vanquisher, would hunt that ghost down and *prove* it was the real culprit. I'd do it if it was the last thing I ever did. And my trusty Stable Boy would help me.

"**Y**ou have a plan, right?" I asked Roger at lunch.

He chewed thoughtfully. I waited on the edge of my seat while my food grew cold. The servants clattered around us, dishing up their food and talking. I'd nabbed a spot in a corner so that we could talk. Gillian was still stuck in the pressing room with Lindy.

Roger took a swig of milk.

"Well?"

"Nope."

"No? What do you mean, no?"

"I mean nope, I don't have a plan," he said. "I'm still thinking."

I slumped down in my seat. I dragged my fork to my mouth. I had no idea what I ate; I just shoveled it in. I'd counted on Roger to help me. I didn't know where else to go.

"Don't look like that; I told you I'd think of something," Roger said.

"When?" I asked. "Her Highness asked me flat out who took that pin and I told her."

Every single freckle on his face popped out in disbelief. "You what?"

"I told her it was the ghost."

"Why'd you go and say a stupid thing like that for?"

"If you could have seen the look in her eye, you'd have told her too."

"What'd she say?"

My eyes stung; I blinked hard.

"Never mind," Roger said. "It's like the Stable Master always says: The bucket has been spilled and that's that. Only thing left to do is scoop up the oats."

"What do oats have to do with anything?" I asked, a quaver in my voice.

I felt a sob rising up. I groped in my pocket for a handkerchief. Something crinkled under my hand. I drew out a white paper with a jagged edge on top. Iago's note. I unfolded it. Inside was a portion of a letter.

Thank you for your advice regarding our unplaced orphans. The child I had in mind, while being well trained, has had difficulties adjusting. We may have to seek a new home for her. Your establishment sounds like an excellent solution. I'll be sure to inform you as soon as I've reached my decision.

Yours truly,
Irene Pepperwhistle

The words *orphans*, *difficulties*, and *solution* flashed before my eyes. Mrs. Pepperwhistle *was* trying to get rid of me.

Numb. The hand holding the paper felt numb. Numbness crept through me until I couldn't feel anything anywhere. I, Darling, the last Wray, was just an orphan who could be sent away.

I thought I'd already lost everything, but maybe I hadn't. Maybe there was more to lose. *Much* more. What would I do without the dresses? And what would they do without *me*?

"What have you got there?" Roger asked, pulling the paper out of my hand.

As he read it, a scowl deepened on his face.

"That's a sneaky, rotten thing to do," he said, and scrunched the paper in his fist.

Visions of orphanages danced before my eyes. Rows of girls lined up for a bowl of gruel. Drafty dormitories. Cold floors. High, cobwebbed ceilings. Bats.

Bats!

Roger waved a hand in front of me. "Are you going to eat that roll?"

I shook my head, clearing it. "I have a plan," I told him, banging my fist on the table.

Roger jumped. And so did everyone around us. I smiled to show everyone that nothing was wrong and then handed Roger my roll.

"Eat up," I said. "You're going to need it."

27

Armed to the hilt, I mounted the stairs to the south tower. I wore my coat *and* my mittens. I carried a candlestick and wielded Marci's longest, thickest darning needle as a weapon. My pockets bulged with nuts I'd wheedled out of the Head Cook, in case our search lasted into the wee hours and we grew faint from hunger. *And* rags tied around the soles of my boots muffled my footsteps. This time the ghost wouldn't hear me coming.

I heard Roger's soft tread behind me. He wore deer-skin boots he'd borrowed from one of the other boys. You couldn't work around horses in them, but he said they were great for hunting. He carried a lantern in one hand and our ghost-trap jar in the other.

The glass squeaked in his grip. It was a tall greenish

jar, the kind the Head Cook stored pickled beets in. We'd argued quite a while over the contents of our jar. The way I saw it, we had one shot at this. This ghost was foxy. Once it saw the trap, it would either take the bait or run. And if the ghost eluded us once, I reckoned it would be smart enough to avoid capture a second time.

Guards stood watch all over the castle, everywhere except the unused south tower. And it just so happened that I'd seen proof of the ghost's presence in that very spot.

The wind moaned in the pitch blackness above us. My candle and Roger's lantern provided the only light. The night was so dark that the big arched window at the top of the stairs was invisible. Marci had long since gone to bed. I'd gone, too, only sneaking out once I'd heard her snore. I'd looked for Iago, but only his little mice children were nestled in my lavender socks. He was out doing whatever mice did late at night.

That hadn't stopped me. I'd have gone alone if I had to.

"Maybe we should have waited for Gillian?" Roger said as we climbed.

I hadn't seen Gillian since morning. Lindy had closeted herself in the pressing room. As far as I knew, she'd held Gillian prisoner at her ironing board until well after supper.

"We have no time to waste. What if Pepperwhistle

makes up her mind in the morning? Then what? It has to be tonight."

"Gillian'll be sore." The glass bottle squeaked in Roger's grip.

"She'll understand. She wouldn't want me to get sent to any dingy old orphanage."

"How do you know it's dingy?"

"Figures it'd be."

Roger grunted in acknowledgment.

I grabbed the post at the top of the stairs and paused. The main landing was as dark as the far side of the cellar. The tiny light radiating from my candle hardly dented it. Roger's lantern cast a glow, but not enough to pierce the gloom. It was a great black night, perfect for luring ghosts out.

"Where should we set our trap?" Roger whispered.

"Here."

"Here? No, higher up. Closer to the bats."

"There aren't any bats."

"Sure there are; I heard them."

"No, you didn't. The squeak that night was me."

"Seriously?"

"I saw something that scared me, so I squeaked. Okay? It happens."

His brown eyes glowed in the candlelight. "What'd you see?"

"Ghost footprints."

"How do you know they were the ghost's?"

"I'll show you."

I let go of the newel-post and slid forward into the room beyond. Roger followed. The other end of the room lay hidden behind a curtain of darkness. My candle's flame lit each step as I placed one foot directly before the other. Roger's light splashed around as the lantern swung in his hand. Last time, our steps had echoed through the dark, but now the silence reverberated in my ears. I itched to hear a sound, any sound.

"There's the wall," Roger whispered.

A vague blankness wavered before me, becoming solid as I approached it. Stepping carefully, I peered down, looking for the footprints.

"There," I said, pointing.

Roger held his lantern out, lighting the blurry prints.

"Wow," he breathed. "They walk right into the wall." He set down his lantern and hunched over the prints.

"This is where we should set up our trap," I said.

"No," Roger said, shaking his head. "We should put the trap where the ghost came in."

"That could be anywhere."

"No, we follow the footprints backward."

I chewed on that. If I stood on the footprints and

walked backward, I'd wind up where I came in. "They lead to the stairs."

"Top of the stairs, then. We'll hide over here and watch." He traced a print with his fingertip.

"Does it come off?"

He held up his finger; it was clean. Well, mostly clean, except for the ground-in grime of working in the stables and a little powdery white dust. He sniffed the dust and sneezed, obliterating whatever had been on his finger.

"Smelled like sour milk," he commented.

"Thanks." I hadn't wanted to know. "Let's get going— it's late."

"I'll leave the lantern here as a marker," he said, taking my candle.

And then he walked back toward the stairs, leaving me in the dark with the ghost's footprints. Not that I was afraid. Nervous, maybe, but not scared. Not really. I crouched down against the wall with one foot in the lantern light and one foot in the dark.

Across the room, I saw his hand place the candle on the floor. Then he took two steps forward and set down the jar.

"How's it look from there?" he said, stepping aside so I could see.

A soft glow lit the tip of the candle, spreading warm

fingers toward a sparkling pile in the bottom of the jar. The sparkles were broken bits of glass we'd mixed into sand.

"Don't put the candle too close. We don't want the ghost to see what's in there, just the sparkle."

He moved the candle a step closer to me, away from the jar.

"Now?"

"Perfect. Get back here."

The candle behind him made a shimmering outline around him as he walked. I shivered at the sight; he looked almost ghostly. He came over and sank down beside me. Then he reached out and turned down the wick on the lantern, extinguishing it. I wished he didn't have to, but it was the only way we could hide in that empty room.

"Do you think it's convincing?" I whispered.

"Looks good to me. That ghost will never know there aren't any diamonds in there unless it gets close enough to look."

"Yeah."

"Think the ghost will fit in that jar? Maybe we should have brought a bigger one."

"No, this is good. Ghosts are vapor; they don't need much space."

"Sure."

"We should be quiet."

"Right."

We sat side by side in the dark and waited. We waited while the candle burned down and the cold seeped out of the wall behind us and into our backs. The only sounds were the moaning of the wind outside the window and Roger's breathing. My head drifted to my chest. My heavy eyelids slid down. . . .

"Hear that?" Roger spoke in my ear.

"What?" I sat up.

The candle burned close to the floor; it was almost used up. My feet were blocks of ice. My fist gripped the darning needle, too frozen to turn it loose.

"Shh."

Six and seven, a distant voice mumbled.

My knees turned to water. The voice did *not* come from the stairs. It came from behind the walls.

"Oh my—" I began.

An echo bounced off the walls.

Roger clamped a hand over my mouth.

"It's behind that wall over there. On the other side of the room," he whispered.

"We have to g-get out of here," I gasped.

I broke free and scrambled to my feet. Roger jumped up and caught me.

"No!" he breathed in my ear. "Listen. We need to lure it out into the room. So we're going to talk, all friendly-like. So it's curious enough to come out for a look."

"Are you crazy?" I whispered back. "It will see us and then—" My throat closed up; I couldn't imagine what then.

"No, it will see the light and then the jar and go over there."

He pulled me back toward the wall and down to the floor. I slumped into my spot by the extinguished lantern. Had he brought matches? I hadn't asked before, and now, watching the last flickering beam of the candle, I wasn't sure I wanted to know.

"Good thing nobody knows we put the jewels here," he said loudly, in a forced cheerful voice.

I sat there glued to the wall. He nudged me in the ribs.

"G-good thing," I sputtered.

"No one will find them here."

"N-no one," I said.

The ghost stopped muttering. Silence filled the room, squeezing all the air out of my lungs. A board creaked in the distance. Maybe the ghost *was* coming up the stairs, after all. Maybe it wouldn't see us, and maybe it would. Two rats caught in our own trap, with nowhere to run but toward the ghost!

The candle across the room sputtered out.

I scrambled along the wall, desperate for somewhere else to go, and dropped the darning needle. It rolled away into the darkness. I wrenched off one of my mittens and groped after it. I felt the baseboard and ran my fingers over it. And then I felt a dip, as if the baseboard sank inward. Odd. It had looked solid enough the other night.

Well, as solid as it could in the lantern light. Maybe the needle had rolled in there. I probed it. Another creak echoed from the stairs.

"It's coming," Roger whispered.

I dug in the hollow, frantic to find my needle.

The baseboard fell under my hand as it suddenly gave way. A low growl sounded behind me. And then the whole wall moved.

28

Roger scrambled for the lantern. I heard the scrape of a match. Saw a flare of light. Roger held up the lantern. Behind us, where there had been a wall, there was now an open passage.

"Oh, man," Roger said.

"Hush," I told him, listening hard.

I glanced at the darkness by the stairs. Another creak sounded, closer this time.

Roger was examining the hole with his lantern, running a gloved hand over the baseboard. "It's a secret passage! There's a trigger here, under the baseboard."

"That's nice," I said, still staring at the dark by the stairs.

"Let's check it out!" Roger said, grabbing me.

The passage was every bit as dark as the empty room.

Black wandered off into more black. There was enough black in there to fill a whole other castle. He tugged me into the blackness beyond. Another low growl sounded. The wall slid back into place, closing us off from the empty room in the south tower.

"Wow, look at that! It's set up with a counterweight!" Roger said.

I didn't know what a counterweight was, and right then I did not want to find out. I grabbed Roger and shook him as hard as I could. "Get me out of here!" I screamed at him.

He spun me around and locked a gloved hand over my mouth. "Quiet!" he barked in my ear.

The dark pressed in on me. The smell of horsey-whatever rising from his glove gagged me. He eased the lantern to the ground and held on to me with his other arm.

Through the wall I heard the sharp sound of boots. And then the sound of talking grew louder.

"Up here."

"What is that?"

"A jar full of sand and a burned-down candle."

"Guards," Roger whispered in my ear. "Quiet, we don't want to get caught."

I wanted to smack him, but he was right. The Guards would drag us straight to the Captain. And he would demand answers. I could just imagine how our ghosting story would go over with him, especially since the Princess hadn't believed me.

I heard a chuckle.

"What on earth is that doing here?"

"Pick it up and let's get going."

Scrape. Clink. Stomp. Stamp.

"Shouldn't we look around some more?"

The voices seemed closer.

"The tower is a dead end. If anyone is up there, they'll have to come back down this way. We have too much ground to patrol to waste time looking."

I heard a scrape and the sound of boots plodding across the floor. Their staccato steps echoed on the stair and then quickly died away.

Roger let me go. Light filtered up from the lantern, highlighting his features.

"What are we going to do?" I rubbed my cold hand against my mittened one. "I lost my mitten on the other side of the wall!"

"We'll get it tomorrow," Roger said, as if that would be the easiest thing in the world. "For now we're going to follow this passage and see where it leads."

"We have to figure out how to open it back up!"

"Darling, I don't think we can open it. I couldn't find a lever."

I felt a scream rising up inside me. Roger must have seen it, because he shook me.

"You don't build a way into a passage without makin' a way out. We'll find the way out."

"But dragons built the castle," I said, "and they're sneaky, horrible creatures. It'd be just like them to build a way in without a way out."

"Dragons might have built the castle, but the finishing work on the inside was done by men. People put this passage here."

"Are you sure?"

"I'm sure." He sounded sure. "Now, it might be tricky, so stay close."

"Okay." I took a deep breath. Magnificent Wray had designed this castle. And dragons couldn't have made the passage. They were too big to fit inside it.

Roger stooped down and picked up the lantern. Then, holding it out in front, he inched away. I followed so closely I practically walked in his shoes. If I'd thought it was dark before, in the passage I entered a whole new realm. Black pressed around me, hovering over me and squeezing me. Black loomed at my side and slinked around my boots. It sucked all the light and air out of the world. I couldn't see anything but a slice of Roger illuminated by the lantern.

I walked on a floor concealed by darkness, surrounded

by walls and a ceiling I couldn't see, heading into yet more darkness. The black was so thick that it took on the appearance of a solid wall around me. We came to a bend in the passage and rounded it.

My eyes ached from straining. Spots and flashes of light swarmed around my head. I knew they weren't real; my eyes were playing tricks on me, trying to make sense of all the blackness. I caught myself holding my breath and exhaled.

The air smelled funny—dusty and moldy at the same time. I wondered if that was even possible. If the passage was dry enough to be dusty, was it also wet enough to be moldy? Pictures of slimy walls and floors covered in dirt and dried-up dead spiders rose in my mind; I pushed them away. Gulping down stale air, I walked with one hand out, as Jane always did.

Was this what it felt like to be Jane? Lost and frightened in a world of black?

"Say something," I told Roger.

"Something," he replied.

"Funny, very funny," I said, the sound of my voice swallowed by the dark.

"Wait," he said, jerking to a stop.

"What is it?" I asked. Like I wanted to know what exciting new horror lurked in the blackness ahead.

"Stairs." Roger felt the dark beside him. "There's a wall here. You should keep a hand on it so you don't fall off."

"Fall off what?"

"I don't see any railing, but the stairs touch the wall, so we'll stay close to it."

He stepped down, and the lantern went down with him. Suddenly, keeping that lantern close meant everything to me. I grabbed the wall and stepped down. My uncovered fingers ached with cold. I tucked that hand in my coat pocket.

Walking on a flat surface when you can't see anything is one kind of adventure; walking down stairs when you can't see where they're taking you is another. My knees wobbled. The steps were narrow and steep. I took them one at a time, finding the next step with my foot and testing it before stepping down.

A *crunch* rang out beneath Roger's boot. I stood still.

"What was that?" I asked.

Roger knelt down on the narrow step, holding the lantern close to something glistening in the dark.

"Wow," he said. He held the lantern out into the black. "Wow, I've never seen one of these before."

"One what?" I said.

"Come down here and see."

Keeping a grip on the wall, I inched down to his step. Roger glanced up, lantern light hitting his chin and casting the rest of his face in shadow. I hunched down next to him and looked. There lay an object that glimmered with the same gleam of the Princess's pearls. Dark shadows clung to it, like cobwebs or lace. I reached out and poked it. The shadow lace disintegrated at my touch.

"Down there," Roger said, pointing with the lantern.

An oval of light fell over a cluster of pearly objects scattered down the steps. More strings and bits of black clung to them. I stared, trying to make sense of what they could be, when I saw it—sitting at the edge of the light, gleaming and bare. Two black holes stared out at me from its pearly whiteness.

"It's—it's—it's—" I sputtered.

"A skull," he said.

An empty skull that once upon a time had belonged to a living person.

"Those are—" I gasped, pointing to the cluster of objects.

"Bones," he added. "It's a whole skeleton." He let out a low whistle.

"That's a dead person! What's a dead person doing here?"

"Probably fell down the stairs in the dark," Roger offered.

I felt sick to my stomach. "*We* could have fallen down these stairs," I said.

"But we didn't," Roger answered. "It clears up one thing, though."

"What?" There was nothing clear about being hunched down on a black staircase in the middle of the darkest darkness that ever existed.

"It explains how the old woman in the story disappeared, never to be seen again."

"Oh." He was right; it had to be her. Poor lady.

"That's why she haunts this place," Roger added. "She can't get buried like she should be."

"What makes you think dead folks want to be buried?"

"Trust me, the dead want to be tucked into a nice dry coffin and put someplace safe."

"That's ridiculous."

He stood; I leaped up with him. He held out a gloved hand.

"Here, it'll be easier to get over it together," he said.

I took his hand and walked with him, stepping when he stepped, stopping when he stopped. I gingerly avoided each bone and every scrap of what had been a dress. A glimmer of gold hugged the base of the skull. A necklace, I guessed. But I didn't reach down to pick it up. The old lady probably wouldn't appreciate my taking it. She seemed to have a thing for jewelry—she'd taken the emerald pin and flung all those other pieces around Princess Mariposa's floor that day.

When we reached the bottom of the stairs, I let go of Roger's hand. After that, there were no more steps; the floor sloped downward and wound around corners. It trailed on and on until it reached a blank wall.

"Hang on," Roger said, holding the lantern aloft.

A rusty iron handle stuck out of the stone. He reached up and pulled on it. The blackness rolled aside, and we tumbled out into a room. A flickering light glowered in a hearth. The smell of baked bread and spices hung in the air.

We had stumbled into the castle kitchens. The wall to the passage behind us slid shut.

29

"Hurry along," Marci said through the hanging scarf that divided the room.

I stood in my underthings, dress in hand. The hem bore streaks and smudges from the previous night's adventure. I'd rubbed at them, but I'd only made them worse. Those passages hadn't been too clean. I'd spent forever the night before combing cobwebs out of my hair. I didn't remember seeing any, but then again, I hadn't seen much of *anything*. At least my stockings were dark and my apron had been protected by my coat—which was a sorrier sight than my dress.

Ann would tattle on me to Mrs. Pepperwhistle before I could finish breakfast. My stomach flip-flopped at the thought. This would probably convince Mrs. Pepperwhistle to send me to the orphanage.

"Darling?" Marci called.

I chewed my lower lip. Maybe if I tied my apron over my dress, the stains wouldn't be too noticeable.

The scarf twitched aside and Marci appeared.

"What on earth did you do to that dress?" she demanded.

"Sat on something?" I suggested. *Like the floor in the south tower,* I thought, keeping the details to myself.

She frowned. And then she saw my coat. "Where were you children playing? In the smithy?"

"Nowhere special," I said.

Marci rolled her eyes in disbelief. "Never mind where. Put that on for now," she ordered. "After Her Highness is dressed, we'll see if we can find a clean one. As for that coat—you'll have to beg Selma to help you sponge it. In your free time. *If* you ever have any."

"Yes, ma'am," I said, scrambling into my clothes.

"I thought you'd gained some sense," Marci said. "But I was premature in that opinion. Still daydreaming your way into trouble, I see." She turned away, muttering about playing in refuse piles.

I bit my tongue. I hadn't been daydreaming. She was wrong—there *was* a ghost. And I'd seen the skeleton to prove it. But I couldn't tell her that without explaining how I knew.

L ater, as I brushed a pair of the Princess's suede boots, I was wearing a clean dress. While Marci had dressed the Princess, I'd slipped into the Girls' dormitory and found one. I'd stuffed my soiled dress in the bottom of the laundry basket. Hopefully, it would get washed without raising any questions. The Laundresses were too busy guarding their laundry from intruders to worry about one child's dirty clothes.

Or at least I hoped they were.

Meanwhile, I had more pressing problems.

My eyes wandered around the walls. Were there other secret passages? If so, where were the doorways into them? Here? In the next room? Were there two or three or—

"Good afternoon, Lindy," Marci said, breaking my train of thought. "How are you today?"

Marci sat at her desk, writing letters, ordering items the Princess had requested. Lindy held her smile as if her face might crack.

"Great, great," she muttered.

"Did you decide what to do with that petticoat?" Marci inquired, signing her name with a flourish.

"Petticoat?" Lindy groused, becoming animated. "I'm not a seamstress! What can I do with it?"

"Ask the Head Seamstress for her advice," Marci said.

"She's a wizard with silk. Maybe it can be transformed into something else."

"Such as?"

"There are several yards of fabric there. Perhaps it could be made into a couple of camisoles and a few hand-kerchiefs."

Lindy huffed at that. "I can't sew."

"I'll help," I said.

Lindy snorted. "Like you can whip up camisoles."

"Darling can't do all of it, but if the Head Seamstress gets her started . . . ," Marci said. "You might be amazed at what she can do."

"Can she make anything fit for the Princess?" Lindy demanded.

"If not, you could always use a few things for your trousseau," Marci said. "The Princess said to find some-thing to do with it; she didn't specify what."

Lindy's eyes widened. Suddenly, she shook herself like I've seen horses do.

"Pack of work," she announced, and stalked into the pressing room.

Marci picked up her quill, chuckling to herself.

"What's a trousseau?" I asked.

"Clothes women accumulate for after their mar-riage."

"Is Lindy marrying Captain Bryce?"

"I think that is the plan."

"She's engaged?" I asked, hurt that nobody had told me.

Marci eyed me, dipping her quill in her inkpot. "Not exactly," she said.

"How can you plan to marry someone you're not exactly engaged to?" I asked.

"That's an excellent question, Darling," Marci said. "Now finish those boots."

I raked the boot with my brush. It was no use arguing. If Marci didn't want to answer a question, she didn't. I went back to looking for a likely spot for a secret entrance. I felt I would make more progress if I had more than the four wardrobe room walls to study.

Ann hobbled into the hall, clutching her side and panting. A strand of hair strayed across her forehead; her braid hung unraveling over her shoulder. One of her stockings had slid down to her boot.

"Do you have an emergency?" Marci asked.

"H-Her H-Highness wants her shawl," Ann gasped. "Her, um, her—oh, I forget which one, but she wants it right now and I ran all the way and twisted my ankle—"

"I think I can select an appropriate shawl for Her Highness," Marci replied, rising. "Darling will take it down for me."

"But *I* have to deliver it!" Ann exclaimed. "The Princess wants it double-quick!"

"Then why didn't you send Dulcie?" I asked. "She's the fastest."

"Fat lot you know," Ann snarled, yanking up her stocking.

"Girls!" Marci said. "I'll not have that in here. Ann, go to Mrs. Pepperwhistle and show her that ankle. Darling will deliver the shawl."

Ann began to protest, but Marci cut her off. "Are you going to limp into the throne room with your hair disheveled?"

Ann clutched her dissolving braid, tears in her eyes.

"Run along. I'll take care of it," Marci said in a softer tone.

I raced through the castle, a sapphire-blue shawl folded over my arm. Walls flew by. Ornate, plain, or punctuated by doors and windows, each wall a candidate for a secret opening, a portal into the unseen world of hidden passageways beyond. A world full of ghosts, spiders, bones—maybe even treasure.

I'd drop the shawl off as quick as quick could be and then I'd take my time walking back. That alcove where my ribbon disappeared that night—I'd bet anything a secret door lurked there. I'd sneak a quick look.

The main hall sprawled below me as I trotted down the

stair. Guards stood at the main doors; groups of people clustered around the edges. I slowed my pace. Court day. I'd forgotten. Lords, ladies, and commoners crowded the hall. There'd be no investigating for me. I trudged down to the main floor, the bounce gone from my step.

Over the buzz of conversation, I heard sobbing and looked around for the source.

Two women dragged a small red-haired girl toward the main doors.

"I don't want to go!" the girl wailed.

Dulcie!

I raced to her, throwing an elbow here and there, pushing my way through. Mrs. Pepperwhistle and a woman I didn't know had Dulcie firmly in their grasp.

"Come along," Mrs. Pepperwhistle said. "Don't make a scene."

"You'll be very happy with us, dear," the other woman assured her. "There will be lots of other children to play with."

The orphanage!

Mrs. Pepperwhistle's letter hadn't been about me. Dulcie hadn't been crying because she was homesick. Only orphans went to the orphanage. Her family was dead!

My blood boiled. Dulcie was a Princess's Girl. She was one of us. We were the only family she had.

I barreled into Dulcie and wrapped both my arms around her tiny waist, shielding her with the Princess's shawl. "Let her go!" I yelled. "You child-stealers, let her go!"

At *child-stealers,* the hall fell silent. Everyone stared at Mrs. Pepperwhistle and her orphanage friend.

"Darling, stop this at once!" Mrs. Pepperwhistle hissed.

Dulcie ripped her hands out of the women's grip and latched on to my arms. "I don't want to go, Darling! Don't let them take me!" she sobbed.

"They'll have to drag both of us," I told her. "Get ready to kick and scream. We'll bite 'em if we have to."

Mrs. Pepperwhistle turned purple. The other woman, who had a face wrinkled like a prune, twisted her hands together.

"Guards," the woman called. "I say, Guards, remove this child."

The Guards at the doors eyed each other uncertainly; they weren't supposed to leave their post. Then the crowd parted and Prince Sterling made his way through.

"Something amiss, ladies?" he asked.

The prune woman gaped up at the Prince. He wore a royal-blue jacket crossed with a garnet sash; a ceremonial sword hung at his waist.

"Who are you, sir?" she said.

"Prince Sterling, this is Mrs. Lavish, Superintendent of

the Orphaned Children's Home," Mrs. Pepperwhistle said. "She's here to take charge of one of the castle's orphans."

"An orphan wearing the Princess's livery?" he asked.

Mrs. Pepperwhistle blushed. "It's a long story," she said hastily. "I'd be happy to explain it all to you later. For now, let's—"

"She hasn't done anything wrong!" I insisted. "You don't lock up innocent little girls."

The crowd around us muttered their disapproval. They pressed closer, as if ready to pounce on the child-stealing women.

"Nobody is locking anybody up," Mrs. Lavish said in a clipped tone.

"She's had difficulties," Mrs. Pepperwhistle explained, eyeing the crowd. "She'll be better off in the orphanage."

"Prince Sterling," I said, "don't let them take her. She's done nothing. Nothing!"

"I don't call hiding all over the castle, being disheveled, and sobbing uncontrollably nothing," sniped Mrs. Pepperwhistle.

"If you'd lost your whole family, you'd sob too," I shot back.

"Good gracious, it is court day! Must we have all this commotion?" a voice demanded.

A hand bearing a silver-topped cane swept people

aside as the Baroness Azure strolled into our midst. Prince Sterling smothered a grin at her approach.

"What on earth is going on out here? We can hear this fussing in the throne room!" she said.

"We're escorting a child to the orphanage," Mrs. Lavish began.

"Who asked you?" Lady Kaye demanded. "Pepperwhistle, explain yourself. What are you doing dragging my ward about?"

"Y-your ward?" Mrs. Pepperwhistle gasped.

"Yes, mine. Her late parents were my tenants. The whole family succumbed to the fever; she's all that's left. I've taken a personal interest in her welfare."

"She's had a great many difficulties," Mrs. Pepperwhistle said.

"Such as?"

"Hiding, refusing to wear proper underclothes, sobbing, hysterics—"

"Has she committed any crime?" Prince Sterling asked.

"Well, no, but I can't have disorder among the Girls."

"It seems to me you've tolerated a great deal of disorder in the past," Lady Kaye said, eyeing me. "Darling, turn her loose."

Mrs. Pepperwhistle tugged at her collar, the picture of embarrassed bewilderment. I let Dulcie go, rescuing the shawl and smoothing out the wrinkles. Dulcie blinked up at the Baroness, rubbing away her tears with her fist.

"Now then," Lady Kaye said in a quiet voice, "have you had difficulties, my dear?"

"Uh-huh," Dulcie said.

"Sobbing and so forth?"

Dulcie nodded, red-faced. A woman in the crowd clucked her tongue and murmured about poor little chicks. I handed Dulcie my handkerchief, one of Marci's mauve-colored cotton ones.

"She'll be happy in the orphanage, and we'll find a new family for her," Mrs. Lavish protested.

"We're her family," I said.

"Do you think you can settle down if you stay here?" Lady Kaye asked Dulcie.

"I want to stay with Darling." Dulcie grabbed my arm. "I'll be good, I promise."

"She will be," I added. "Extra good. She's the fastest runner the Princess has. We need her. Ann twisted her ankle running up for this!" I held up the shawl, which I remembered the Princess had been waiting on for some time.

"In that case, Dulcie, you should deliver that shawl to Her Highness," the Baroness said with a twinkle in her eye.

I handed Dulcie the shawl and she was off, messy braids flying, petticoat-free skirt glued to her legs. Mrs.

Lavish watched her go with a grimace of disapproval. Mrs. Pepperwhistle had recovered herself and was tidying her bun.

"Thank you, Mrs. Lavish, that will be all," Mrs. Pepperwhistle said.

With a *humph*, Mrs. Lavish bowed and took her leave, walking stiff-backed to the doors.

"Good riddance," I muttered under my breath.

The Baroness rapped me on the top of my head with her cane's silver knob.

"I've got an eye on you, my girl," Lady Kaye said. "Watch your step."

"Yes, ma'am," I said, rubbing my scalp.

"Go back upstairs now," Mrs. Pepperwhistle said in a tone that suggested she'd deal with me later.

30

"The Baroness is watching me," I told Gillian at supper.

"Maybe you should try staying out of trouble for a while," she said, toying with a curl.

I gaped at her. What was I supposed to do? Let them steal Dulcie? Give the ghost free rein to ruin my life? Stand back and forfeit the Princess's good opinion?

Roger slid next to me on the bench. He wore a buff-colored leather cap. He grinned at me.

"You're a First Stable Boy!" I said. "That was quick; the Stable Master must have been impressed."

"Yep. Got charge of Lady Marguerite's horses."

"That's nice," Gillian said.

"Horses?" I said.

"Two." He held up two fingers. "You know what that means?" His grin widened.

"No," Gillian said.

"It means that when Lady Marguerite don't ride, it's my job to exercise her horses for her."

"And she's got two," I said. "You'll get to ride most days! That's great."

Nodding, he turned pink with pleasure.

"Wonderful," Gillian chirped at Roger. And then she turned back to me. "The Baroness is a wonderful person," she added.

"You two chums, then?" Roger asked, pulling off his cap. He laid it on his lap; my missing mitten lay stuffed inside its crown.

Gillian frowned, winding a curl around her finger.

"I didn't say she wasn't; I said she's watching me," I protested.

Under the table, Roger slid the mitten out of his hat and onto my lap. I grabbed it and stuffed it in my pocket. It caused an unseemly bulge in my apron; I'd worry about that later.

"The Baroness is too important to bother about children," Gillian said.

"She tells *you* stories," I argued. "What are you? An old lady?"

"That's different," Gillian said, waving my comment away. "I listen."

"You really think this is all my fault, don't you?" I said.

"Of course not," Gillian said. "But you could try staying out of trouble. Then maybe someone will promote you."

My face burned. Gillian wouldn't be where she was if I hadn't gotten into trouble.

"I'll remember that if anyone tries to drag *you* off," I said.

Gillian turned to Roger. "Well? Don't you have anything to say?"

"Never met her," Roger replied, tucking into his supper.

"Not about the Baroness—about Darling being in trouble!"

"I trust Marci to pound some sense into her," Roger said with a shrug.

Gillian scooted off her bench and grabbed her tray.

"There's no talking to the two of you," she said, flouncing off.

Roger watched her go, an amused gleam in his eye.

"Now that we got rid of her, we can talk," he said.

"I wasn't trying to get rid of her!"

"Were you going to tell her about the passage?"

I stewed over that, crumbling my roll onto my casserole.

"I didn't think so," Roger said. "But now we need to figure out what other passages exist."

"You think there are more?"

"I bet this whole place is like one giant anthill full of secret tunnels. We just need to figure out where the doors are."

"I've been thinking," I said, and told him my theory.

We strolled across the main hall soon after supper. Servants and nobles rambled here and there, but most were preoccupied with their own business. The nobles were on their way to the main dining room, and the servants pursued their errands. Guards stood at attention. No one paid any attention to us; I carried a covered basket and looked purposeful.

I figured that if secret doors existed right under their noses, then most of them weren't very observant. We aimed to arrive at the alcove about the time dinner was served to the Princess. The main hall and the corridors leading to it were emptiest then.

I tripped up to the little table by the alcove where my ribbon had disappeared and placed my covered basket on the floor. I stood directly in front of the niche. Roger slipped behind me. I made a big face at my bootlaces. Then

I bent over and arduously retied both of them. Roger sank to the floor and began searching under the mirror for the hidden door's trigger.

A quiet *snick* sounded behind me. Roger tugged on my apron. With a quick glance around, I scooped up the basket and ducked through the hole in the wall. Roger waited on the other side, grabbing the lever and shutting the door.

The wall slid closed. We'd done it! We'd found another hidden passage.

I yanked the cloth off the basket and dug out our scrounged-up supplies.

"Here you go," I said, handing Roger one of the two carriage lamps he'd procured.

Not only were they small and lightweight, but each one boasted a tin reflector. We could curl our hands around their leather straps and point the light wherever we wanted it to shine.

Next, I handed Roger the matches. He struck one on the bottom of his boot and raised the glass shield to light my lamp candle. Because they were thicker than regular candles, the squat lamp candle would burn the same length of time. Roger had calculated that we had two hours to explore. The lantern held oil and would burn longer, but it was bulky and heavy. If caught in tight quarters with a pin-stealing, room-wrecking ghost, we wanted to be able to maneuver with ease.

I loaded my pocket with chalk and string. Then I handed Roger the pocketknife. I slipped my locket under my apron's bodice—no sense alerting this jewelry-happy ghost to its presence. Then I folded the cloth into a triangle and tied it over my hair to keep it clean. Roger wore his cap. I tucked the basket into a cranny by the wall and dusted off my hands. We'd decided that carrying the basket would slow us down and that we could sneak back to rescue it from behind the wall later.

"I'm ready," I said.

Roger shined his lamp around the narrow space. Cobwebs drifted down from the ceiling. Dust powdered the floor. The passage led a few paces back and then up a stair.

"Here we go." Roger set off.

I followed, flashing my handy lamp around, ready to squash any spider I saw. The steps were lower and wider than the ones before, easier to climb. As we went up, I tried to imagine where we were in relation to the outside. But I quickly lost my way as the steps ended and a new corridor appeared. It took several sharp turns. Light broke in from time to time, spilling between cracks and crevices, brightening our way for a moment before the next stretch of passage engulfed us in darkness. We wound around and up and beyond. And up again.

We reached a split where three openings led in different directions. Roger picked the one on the right, and I marked it with a big chalk X.

"Have you figured out what you're going to say to the ghost?" Roger asked.

"Mostly," I answered, shining my light on a funny rippled spot on the wall. "What's this?"

Roger ran his light over it. An iron knob glistened on a support beam.

"Whoa! Found one!" he hooted. He reached for the knob, and I stopped his hand.

"We don't know where that comes out or who might be behind it," I said.

He wrinkled his forehead, his freckles swarming together.

"We should find the ghost first," I reminded him.

"But—"

"We can open it later."

He dropped his hand. I stepped back. His fist darted out and punched the knob. The funny slice of wall rolled open. The outline of a bed blocked our path. Two kids gawked at us from across the darkened room.

Roger yelped.

"It's us in a mirror," I told him, "in a boring, empty bedroom." I punched the knob and shut the wall. "Satisfied?"

I borrowed the pocketknife and cut a bit of string to tie on the knob.

"Everyone's at dinner; this is the perfect time to open doors," Roger argued.

"Find the ghost," I said. "Convince it to cooperate. Then, I promise, we will open every last one."

"You'll be afraid of getting caught." He tugged at his cap the way he always did when he was angry.

"Nope, I won't." I crossed my heart. "It might get me in trouble, *but* it's not like I haven't been in trouble before."

He rolled his eyes and started off again. Down a stair, around a corner, under an arch we walked. Our lamp candles had dwindled to the half point. Anytime the way split, I marked our choice. Roger whistled under his breath as he strolled along.

At one spot, we found a wide space like a little room or a large closet. Roger's light glanced off a metal object. He sucked in his breath. A partially used-up candle sat in an elaborate brass candlestick on the floor.

"How'd that get in here?" he asked.

"Someone left it, probably ages ago."

He ran his light up and down it.

"It don't look too dusty."

"Neither is the floor," I said, waving my light across his boots. "There aren't many places for dust to come through. And you know how fussy the Maids are."

"I don't like it." Roger chewed his lip.

"Want to quit and go back?"

"Not enough candle left," he said. "If *you're* quitting, then you need to find a door to open."

It was the one flaw in our plan. If we didn't find the ghost before we ran out of light, we'd have to bail out wherever we could. And who knew where that might be? It was dicey: pick a random secret door to pop through and hope no one was waiting on the other side.

I'd sort of hoped we'd run into the ghost in time to head back the way we'd come. But the more we climbed up and down and wound around and around, I knew that wasn't going to happen. We'd have to take our chances at some point. I hoped we wouldn't land in some nasty place, like Mrs. Pepperwhistle's room.

"Good thing that ghost didn't see our trap. We might have gotten off on the wrong foot that way," Roger said.

"We weren't trying to hurt it," I said, conscious that the ghost could be listening. "We just want to talk to it."

Roger wore a puzzled frown for a moment, and then he winked.

"Yeah, if only it would talk to us. Get to know us," he agreed.

"We could use its help," I added.

Silence. A dust mote wandered through my lamp's beam. With a shrug, we set off again.

"There are miles of these things," I said as we walked. "It'd takes ages to learn your way around them."

"We'll have to figure out how to lay up a supply of candles. I can't keep swiping them. It'll get noticed," Roger said.

"You swiped them?"

"No, Darling, my fairy stable mother give 'em to me."

"Roger," I said, stopping suddenly. "Do you have one? A mother, I mean?"

"Sure."

"I mean, living like."

"Yeah, she lives in a mill by a river. My uncle is the miller."

"You never talk about her."

"Nothing much to say."

I sighed. Sometimes Roger could be downright irritating.

"Look." He pointed with his lamp.

The passage ended in a *T*. One branch went right and one went left.

"We should split up," he said.

"We agreed to stay together."

He gestured with his lamp. "Burning low. We'll have to get out soon. It might be better if we picked different doors. We'd learn where there were two doors instead of only one, and maybe one of us wouldn't get caught."

So far the passages had been dusty and cobwebby but reasonably warm and dry. There hadn't been any steep stairs or sharp drops. Other than confronting the ghost alone, the only real danger was when we went back out.

"Okay. Pick," I said.

"Left."

"See you at lunch tomorrow?"

"Sure," Roger said, and tipped his cap. "We'll trade stories then."

I headed off, swinging my lamp from side to side, eager to find a door. I wouldn't tell Roger for anything in the world, but the sooner I got out, the better. I'd had enough dark spaces to last me for a while. I walked on until I found a stair leading down.

The stair wound like a snake, leveling off for a brief space before recommencing. The air grew colder and damper. My candle began to sputter. I would have turned around, but my legs trembled from exhaustion. I didn't think I could climb back up. I figured I must be near the kitchens again, and I was looking forward to a nice warm hearth.

And then the stair ended and the passage sloped down. I crept forward, raking the walls with my light, searching for a lever. Ahead, the passage came to a dead end. What now?

I combed the lichen-covered dead-end wall with my light. It sparkled on a rusty chain hanging from the ceiling. With a deep breath, I stretched up and yanked on it.

The wall rattled and then cranked aside, revealing a black void. I stepped out. The wall closed behind me. I squinted, wondering where in the castle this could be—and how much longer my candle would last.

Then I saw it.

A wavering shape lingered in the air before me. I was all alone in a dark hole somewhere in the castle. No one knew where I was. There was nowhere to run. Nowhere to hide. And worst of all, no one to hear me scream.

"Yipe!" I squeaked.

That's when the ghost reached out and grabbed me.

31

The hand that held me wasn't filmy or foggy; it was solid. It yanked me so hard that my boot heels scraped the stone beneath me. Arms flailing, I tumbled into its grasp, dropping my carriage lamp. The ghost snorted in surprise.

It pulled me close. Fringe tickled my face. The smell of unwashed socks assaulted my nose. The hand holding me felt icy cold through the fabric of my sleeve.

"Walk," a hoarse voice barked in my ear.

The ghost's breath stunned my senses with its rotten-egg odor. It loosed me only to knuckle me in the middle of my back, propelling me forward into the darkness. I walked with my hands out before me, feeling my way. I heard the tap of my boots on stone. As my eyesight adjusted, I noticed shapes—racks of bottles. I was on the dark side of the cellar, where the cold kept the vegetables chilled and no one went unless they had to.

The fist at my back turned me so that I walked behind the racks and onto hard-packed dirt. Ahead, I saw the faint glimmer of a light. A hoard of broken bits of furniture blocked my path. I tripped over a table leg. The ghost yanked me upright and prodded me on. I headed for the light like a moth to a flame. Behind an old carved wardrobe, I saw a grimy blanket hung like a tent over a lit lantern. The ghost's camp.

Only by this time, I'd figured out that my ghost wasn't a phantom in the normal sense of the word. I strained over my shoulder to get a better look at it, only to be shoved headlong into the blanket tent.

"What are you doing in my parlor?" the voice asked.

"Nothing," I said, dusting myself off and looking at my captor.

A tall figure with a white fringed shawl pulled up over her head confronted me. She pulled off the shawl and draped it over a backless chair. A deathly pale woman with a dirty face, bedraggled hair, and a soiled, patched dress stared at me with intense blue eyes.

"Cherice!" I gasped.

I gawped at the former Wardrobe Mistress. She'd vanished once her plot with the imposter Dudley had been exposed. The castle and its grounds had been thoroughly searched, but she'd eluded capture. "What are you doing down here?"

When she answered, her voice changed, the way I'd heard it do once before. It became cultivated and smooth, a lady's voice, not the coarse tones of a moment before.

"Hello, Darling," she said. "Welcome to my little cottage in the woods."

She gestured with a surprisingly well-manicured hand, which was at odds with the rest of her appearance. I sat on the stool she'd indicated, puzzling out her sudden appearance. Her "cottage" contained backless chairs, rickety stools, a bed made of straw, and an assortment of tins and wooden crates.

And a collection of items I recognized: Marci's scissors and pincushion, a nail file that someone—I couldn't remember who—had complained about missing, and a host of other objects, including the shawl Cherice had been wearing. The Head Laundress, Selma, had complained that her best shawl had gone missing. From the look of it in the light, it hadn't fared well with its new owner.

Cherice was a thief, and a distinctly bad-smelling one at that. Then I realized that she was more than a magpie collecting trinkets.

"You took the Princess's pin and put it in Francesca's boot!" I said.

Cherice laughed, settling herself on a crate and

arranging her skirt in what would have been attractive folds if it hadn't been so filthy. The last time I'd seen that dress—on the day of Princess Mariposa's canceled wedding—it had been bright pink. Now it was more of a cinnamon color.

"Francesca deserved every bit of it, my dear," Cherice cooed. "I thought that was one of my better tricks." She fingered the magnifying glass she'd always worn swinging from its chain around her neck.

"It sure got me in trouble," I said.

"How so?"

"Everybody thought I did it to get back at her. You cost me my post as a Princess's Girl with that *trick*."

She blinked furiously, as if confused. "No," she said, "I righted that wrong. Just like I'll right all the others."

She dug in her sleeve and produced a small silver object she polished between her fingers. Her once-dainty smile twisted into a grimace.

"What wrongs?" I asked, fidgeting on the stool.

A gleam lit her eyes. "The long-ago wrongs done by the wicked ones."

Her tone had shifted again, losing its cultivated air. Her polishing motion quickened.

"You wrecked the Princess's bedroom," I said, realizing that she was behind the trouble in the laundry, too.

"Y-yes," she snickered. "Let her know what it's like to have what belongs to you trampled underfoot."

I struggled to make sense of what she said.

"Do you mean Dudley?" I guessed.

"No," she said with a snort. "I'm rid of *him.* I'll have someone much finer once I've gotten back what's mine."

"Wh-what did you want to get back?" I asked with a growing unease.

She'd tried to steal the King's talisman and loose the dragons. Was that what she had hung around for these past months, hiding, using the passages to spy and steal?

"My inheritance," Cherice said, leaning forward.

"Oh," I said as if her response were perfectly clear. "Good luck with that."

She studied me, winding a lock of soiled blond hair around her free hand. The one holding the object slid into the folds of her skirt. A secretive, sly look crossed her face. "You're not one of them, are you, Darling?"

She was as crazy as a Cook stirring an empty pot. And dangerous. She'd always been kind to me in the past, but the image of the ransacked bedroom hung in my mind's eye. As Jane had said, that act had been vicious. And Cherice had been ready to dispatch me once before, when she thought I was a spy. But I'd been wearing a dress, so she hadn't actually known it was *me* who'd overheard her plotting.

Now did not seem like a good time to bring that up. I glanced around, looking for a quick way out. I heard a faint scuttling. Probably the rats Francesca insisted were not allowed in the castle. Too bad they weren't acquaintances of Iago's. I could've used a mouse hero right then.

Absolutely no one knew where I was. It had to be late in the evening. Everyone would be going to bed. Roger was either stuck in the passages, back in the stable, or answering questions from the Guards. I suddenly wished it were dinnertime and some Footman would come looking for a bottle of wine to serve.

That wasn't likely to happen.

If I was quick, I might jump up and bash Cherice over the head with the stool I was sitting on. Stun her, maybe. Then race through the maze of stored goods to the stairs.

I squirmed; I wasn't at all sure I could find my way in the dark without getting lost. There was plenty of distance to cover, which would allow her time to pick herself up and come after me.

"She didn't answer," Cherice whispered to herself. "Maybe she's lying. Maybe she's not my friend."

"Sure, I'm your friend," I said. "You were good to me."

"How did you know about the secret doors?" she demanded, the clouds in her eyes clearing.

"I didn't," I said. "I was just playing around and found one."

Her eyes narrowed to a slit. Quick as a striking hawk, she grabbed my apron and hauled me off my stool.

"You had a light," she snarled. "You weren't playing around. You were looking for something. What was it?"

"A g-ghost?" I said, knees knocking. "I thought the castle was haunted."

That was the wrong thing to say. She shook me so hard my brain rattled in my skull. My apron tore and my locket spilled out. The starburst engraving blazed in the dim light. At the sight of it, she hissed like a snake. She released me to grasp the locket, yanking me forward by its chain. "Where did you get this?" she said through gritted teeth.

"It was m-my mother's," I gasped as the chain bit into my neck.

"Liar!" she shrieked. "This was the Wrays'!"

"My mother was a Wray," I said in a strangled voice.

Momentarily, she loosened her hold, staring straight into my face. "It could be," she whispered. "You're fair; you have the aquamarine eyes. You could be one of us."

I studied the dirty face; Cherice was fair, too, and pretty—just how Warden Graves had described my mother. Could *she* be a Wray? All the things she'd done—trying to

279

release the dragons, hiding, spying, ruining the Princess's things—fit into a pattern. But the castle didn't seem to know her like it knew me. She hadn't known about the magic.

More important, she didn't know that I knew.

"You said you're looking for your inheritance," I said cautiously, seizing on my chance to get away. "Maybe I can help; my mother was the last Wray. Maybe—"

"I AM THE LAST WRAY!" Cherice shouted. "THE INHERITANCE IS MINE!"

I was too stunned to speak. She hurled me against a nearby broken chair. It collapsed under my weight, splintering to pieces. The fall knocked the air out of me. I lay breathless for a moment until I saw Cherice looming over me with a wild look in her eyes. I groped for one of the broken chair parts. As I did, I twisted slightly and saw two familiar eyes stare at me through a crack in an old cupboard.

Dulcie crouched behind the broken boards, peeking in. A telltale streak glistened on her cheek.

"Get—" I hesitated. The Guard room was a long way away. "Get the Laundresses! Run!"

At that, Dulcie popped up out of her hiding place and shot into the darkness.

Cherice roared in rage, snatching me off the ground like a bag of onions. She grabbed hold of my locket again and began dragging me by it, throwing furniture out of her way as if it were made of kindling.

"I have a place for you," she snarled.

With a sick sensation, I knew exactly which place she had in mind. *The passages.* She'd had months—maybe years, counting the time she'd spent as Wardrobe Mistress—to unravel their mysteries. Once she got me in there, it'd be a long, long time before anyone found me. Even if Roger became worried and went looking, it might be days or weeks before he stumbled on the right place.

I'd never last that long!

The glimmer of lantern light had become lost in the jumble of wine racks. I heard the crunch of stone under my boot and knew the door wasn't far away. I fought like a wild thing, biting and clawing. Cherice tightened her grip on my locket and slugged me in the stomach. I doubled over, choking as the taut chain jerked my head up. I felt it tear my skin as it gave way and I fell.

The stone rushed up to meet me, slapping my head so hard my ears rang. I heard Cherice standing over me, panting. Something warm oozed down my neck.

"You made me break it," she said in disbelief.

I heard the tinkling of metal objects hitting the floor. Then she lunged for me and wrapped her hands around my throat. I bucked, but I couldn't throw her off. She squeezed. My eyes bulged. Frantic, I flailed around for something, anything, I could use against her. There was nothing—nothing but air and stone.

"You broke it! You broke it!" she howled.

My lungs screamed for air. My head felt like it would burst. I dug my fingers into the cellar's paving stones. And there, bubbling like an unseen brook, the castle's magic tickled my fingertips.

Magic! Warm and sweet, it rippled up under my hand. And it spoke to me. *Let us in,* it said, tapping at my palm.

I pawed into it, pulling it out of the floor and letting it course through me. It sang in my veins, hummed in my bones, welling up until it reached my skin. And then it flared like a flame, lashing out at Cherice. Magic bolted into her like a white-hot poker. She let go, crying out and falling backward.

I heard her hit the floor. I heard her whimpering. I sucked in great breaths of air. The tickle of magic lingered inside me. *It had saved me.*

Darling, move, the magic whispered as it faded away. Until only a reassuring echo remained.

I scrabbled around on the stone, trying to push myself up. My fingers found metallic objects—my locket and chain and something else. A key. I scraped them both up, crammed them in my pocket, and staggered to my feet. I strained in the dark, deciding which way to run, when I heard Cherice sobbing.

If I left right then, I might be able to reach the stairs before her wits revived and she chased me. *But.* She might not do that. She might run for the hidden door. If she made it back into the passages, I'd be right where I started from: without the ghost, without proof, without the possibility of clearing my name.

I saw the dim outline of her lying on the ground. I, Darling the-last-Wray Fortune, walked over and *sat* on Cherice like a queen on her throne. She groaned with my weight on her stomach. I elbowed her for quiet.

"You're not getting away this time," I told her in a voice raspy from choking.

In the distance, I saw a flash of light and heard the pounding of boots.

"Over here," I croaked as loudly as I could. "I've got her!"

32

A phalanx of Laundresses, wielding heavy paddles, burst upon us. Selma led the charge, waving a lantern over her head like a banner.

"Circle 'em, gals!" she cried.

In a twinkling, a wall of heavy-muscled, red-knuckled, grim-faced Laundresses glared down at us over their paddles. Dulcie squirmed between them, panting. She glowed with excitement.

"I got them," Dulcie said.

"You're the fastest ever," I told her. Then I turned to Selma. "I found out who was causing trouble in the laundry. Cherice!" I hopped up off her and gestured to my prize. "See?"

An incredulous look flooded Selma's features. "I don't

believe it!" she said, surveying Cherice's dirty and disheveled appearance.

Cherice snarled at the Head Laundress, baring her teeth in a ferocious grimace.

"And the cat's got claws, I see." Selma dug in her pocket and pulled out her hankie. "You're bleeding," she said, offering it to me.

I took it, suddenly remembering the warm trickle down my neck, and pressed the cloth to my wound.

"You"—Selma pointed at Dulcie—"run and get the Guards. Tell them the kitty is in the bag."

"Yes, ma'am!" Dulcie crowed, and raced off.

Cherice staggered to her feet, smoothing her ratted and filthy hair.

"You're no master to me. Let me by, you louts," she said, waving her manicured fingers at them.

"Not so fast, my lady. You're the one's been doing mischief to my gals," Selma said.

"And stealing." I pointed toward Cherice's "cabin in the woods." "Back there is a whole lair full of stuff."

"Go see, Urs," Selma said, favoring Cherice with a baleful glare.

Ursula turned in the direction I'd indicated, and, seeing the faint glimmer of the candle, stalked off.

Cherice colored slightly but held her head high.

"Step aside, I say. *I* am the last Wray. You're nothing to me," she said.

"I don't care if you're the long-lost sister of the Baroness Azure!" Selma told Cherice. "You've some answering to do."

"Yeah!" the Laundresses roared, menacing her with their paddles.

"Stop this vulgar display at once," Cherice commanded. She shook out her skirts, dislodging a cloud of dust.

Several of the Laundresses coughed, but Cherice took no notice. She patted the ribbons on her bodice as if reassuring herself. She tossed her soiled locks. "I don't expect women such as yourselves to understand," she purred, "but *I* am royalty."

The Laundresses howled with laughter. Cherice's eyes darkened.

"You let me go or I'll send you all to the dungeons," she cried.

"Oh, no!" Nina gasped. "She'll send us to the drying room!"

The Laundresses chortled with glee.

"Little Missy Upstairs is a-scaring me!" Rayna snorted with derision.

"Tell them, Darling," Cherice demanded. "Tell them who I am!"

They stared at me, surprised.

Uncertainty nibbled at my conscience. Cherice might be related to the Wrays, but she might not. She might just think she was. After all, the magic came to my aid. Not hers.

"She's crazy," I said. "Ask Princess Mariposa. My mother was the last Wray, and now I am. She's an imposter."

Cherice choked with anger.

"Like that fink Dudley," Selma agreed. "Shut your mouth, Cherice, or we'll do it for you."

"Selma, this here's your shawl!" Ursula announced, returning with it draped over her paddle.

Selma took one look and cried, "It's filthy! You, you—I'll get you for this, Cherice." Tears wet her cheeks. "My very best, pure-white shawl."

"I wouldn't sully myself with that rag," Cherice sniffed.

Selma squealed with rage and grabbed the paddle from the Laundress next to her. Cherice threw her hands over her head with a shriek.

Just then a voice rang out through the darkness of the cellar.

"Halt in the name of Her Highness!"

Captain Bryce and his Guards had arrived.

Princess Mariposa paced in her office, a black evening gown trailing behind her. The diamonds on her black shoes sparkled with each step. She worried a silk handkerchief between her fingers. Prince Sterling, Lady Kaye, Marie, the Head Steward, and Mrs. Pepperwhistle all watched her anxiously.

Cherice struggled between two Guards, spitting and snarling like a cat.

"Let me get this straight, Captain," the Princess said. "This *person* has been camping in my cellar, stealing from my servants, and plotting against me all this time?"

Captain Bryce motioned to one of his men. That Guard held the bundled-up and bulging shawl, which he spilled on the carpet. Stolen possessions tumbled out.

"These are the things that have been reported missing," he replied. "All here and accounted for."

"But how? Why didn't anyone see her?"

"Your Highness, she's a sly one," the Captain said with a grimace. "She eluded us."

"I saw her," I said, my voice scratchy.

I pressed the handkerchief to my throbbing neck. Now that the excitement had died down, every inch of me hurt, my neck worst of all. Dulcie clung to my free hand, her flame-colored hair wilder than ever after her race through the castle.

"You said you saw a ghost," the Princess reminded me.

"It was dark. She had that shawl over her head—I thought she *was* a ghost."

"And you just happened to find her in the cellar?" she replied.

"I wasn't looking for her," I said, thinking fast. "I was looking for Dulcie."

I squeezed Dulcie's fingers, willing her to remain silent. The Baroness eyed Dulcie sharply.

"Dulcie wasn't hiding," I added quickly. "I wanted to make sure she was okay."

"Well, in any event, Darling, you've done me a great service," Princess Mariposa said.

"Service!" Cherice shrieked. "You should bow down to me! I'm the one. Serve me!"

"Who are *you*, Cherice?" the Princess asked.

"I'm the one," Cherice said. "It's mine. Mine!"

"What is yours?" Princess Mariposa asked.

"The key," Cherice said, calming down. "It opens doors."

I thought guiltily of the key in my pocket. I didn't mention it; I waited to hear what she might say about it.

"What doors?" the Princess asked, exasperated. "Where?"

"I won't tell you," Cherice purred. "It's mine."

"She's been carrying on like that since we caught her," Captain Bryce said. "She's deranged."

"Yes, well, have your men lock her up for tonight," the

Princess said with a sigh. "You can send her to the asylum in the morning."

"You're not going to try her for her crimes?" the Baroness inquired.

"If you can get a straight answer out of her, be my guest," the Princess said.

For the first time since I'd known her, Lady Kaye had no reply. The Princess waved the Guards away. They left, dragging a thrashing, bawling Cherice every step of the way.

"What a relief, my dear," Lady Kaye said to Princess Mariposa. "We can all rest easier knowing that none of your servants was involved in this sordid business."

The Princess nodded.

"Maybe you can put the past behind you now," Marie said kindly.

"Maybe," the Princess agreed.

I sagged. It was late. The struggle with Cherice had drained me. My arm holding the handkerchief ached. I flexed it, letting my hand fall away from my neck. The cloth was soaked crimson with blood.

"Oh my!" Princess Mariposa exclaimed. "Darling! You're hurt! You're—"

"I'm all right," I said. I clamped the handkerchief back over my neck. But the color had drained from her face. She swayed on her feet.

Prince Sterling reached out and caught her. Then he pulled her close.

"Don't worry, I've caught you," he said. "I won't let you fall."

She gazed up at him a moment, blushing.

And then something wonderful happened. Princess Mariposa looked into the Prince's warm brown eyes and saw what had been as plain as day to the rest of us.

"Yes," she murmured, "I think you have caught me."

And then, to the shock and surprise of everyone, she kissed him.

The Head Steward looked away. The Baroness became very interested in the silver knob of her cane. Mrs. Pepperwhistle eyed the ceiling. Marie groped for her handkerchief, eyes glistening with tears. Captain Bryce stared at his boots.

Me? I looked. I wouldn't have missed it for the world.

The next morning the Herald announced the engagement of Princess Mariposa Celesta Regina Valentina of Eliora to His Highness, Prince Humphrey Frederic Albert Sterling of Tamzin.

I sat on a kitchen bench, throat swathed in bandages, bruised from head to foot, and grinned. Servants surrounded me, celebrating the Princess's upcoming marriage.

"I knew it all the time," Lindy crowed.

"No doubt you did," Marci commented, dropping a spoonful of sugar into her tea.

"Does a body good," the Head Cook said, offering me a steaming cup of hot chocolate.

"Very romantic," the Pastry Chef said, sliding a plate of apple turnovers under my nose.

"Yup," I croaked, barely able to speak. I helped myself to a turnover.

"It's been a long time coming," Jane said, knitting needles clicking.

She'd no sooner finished the mittens and hood for the Head Cook than the Pastry Chef had demanded a set for his wife. Jane knitted away with a gleam in her blurry blue eyes.

"And that Cherice!" Lindy said, flipping her hair over her shoulder. "I always knew she was too good to be true."

"Yeah," the Pastry Chef said. "Tell that part again, Darling."

"And the part about the Princess falling for Prince Sterling," an Under-chopper said.

"And the ghost, don't forget that!" Marci chimed in.

"Tell us *the whole thing* once more," the Head Cook urged.

Chasing the bite of turnover down with a sip of hot chocolate, I broke my own rule not to talk about Her

Highness: I told them about finding Cherice and about the Princess, kiss and all.

Well, almost everything. I left out the dresses and the passages. And the key.

A Kitchen Maid nearly swooned. The Footmen nudged one another.

"I wish I could go to the wedding," Gillian said with a sigh.

Every servant in the room sighed with her.

That evening, I snuck back into the closet. Lyric whistled from his cage. The dresses trembled with excitement. I stood for a moment, savoring it all. The flash of jewels, the shine of silk, the gloss of ribbons—a melody of fabric and lace and *magic*.

The Wrays' magic. And, in a sense, *my* magic. Not only did it fill the dresses and hum in the castle but it had saved me. *Me*, Darling Wray Fortune.

"The Wrays' Darling," I murmured, remembering the reassuring echo in the magic.

The glass canary twinkled at me in the moonlight. There was more to this magic than met the eye. And I had yet to discover what that was. But I would.

"I'm going for a walk," I said, and the dresses rejoiced as only they could, banging their hangers and waving their flounces.

Five, a ruby velvet with satin ribbons, shivered with anticipation. I picked it up and slipped it on. The familiar nip-and-fit whirled around me. In the mirror, a lady with delicate features, a tiny pointed nose, and big blue eyes gazed at me. She wore an iris-blue gown with a rope of pearls around her neck. Her fingers glittered with rings. She seemed almost ready to speak. But that was just my imagination.

I headed off into the castle. Marci had sent my locket to the city for repair, but I hadn't shown the key to anyone. Cherice had claimed that she was the last Wray, but *I* was. I didn't know who she was for sure, but I knew there were answers somewhere.

I paused a moment at the great library doors, gathering my courage before turning the lion's-head knob. Then I opened the door, and the rush of magic from the books assaulted me. They whispered like conspirators, *Read me.* I didn't dare without Her Highness's permission. I hurried past them straight to the locked cabinet that contained the King's collection. Holding my breath, I looked.

The slot where *Magnificent Reflections* had sat was empty.

Of course it was. I'd known it before I looked. Not that Master Varick would make the mistake of letting someone borrow it again. But still, I had to see for myself.

"Her Majesty has that book," Master Varick said softly. "I believe she intends to keep it."

I jumped; I hadn't heard him coming. I turned, plastering a fake smile on my face.

"What book?" I said, pretending not to know.

"Never mind. May I help you find something, Lady Ellen?" Master Varick inquired.

"Just browsing," I said. I knew better than to fall into that trap again.

"If you have any questions . . . ," he said expectantly.

"I was wondering about old families . . . like the Wrays, for example," I said in a casual tone. My heart pounded in my chest.

"The genealogies are in Her Highness's office, I'm afraid," he said. "But you could ask her about them."

"Oh," I said, smile faltering. "Thank you."

I walked back to the doors, past the shelves, reading titles. Hearing the magic hum. With a sigh, I nodded good night to the Head Librarian and left.

I walked back up to the wardrobe hall. Marci sat at her desk, writing.

"Good evening, Lady Ellen. Or should I say *Darling*?" she said, looking up.

"I wasn't doing anything," I told her. "Just trying one on."

"It's a nice night for a stroll," she commented. "Find anything interesting?"

"No," I said. Then one of the questions that had been nagging me burst out. "Marci, can anyone wear a dress?"

She pressed her hands into a steeple, considering. "No, I don't think so."

"You did. I can. Roger can't."

She looked at me a long time before speaking. Then she said, "It's something to do with the magic—it chooses people for its own purposes."

That made sense. I knew why it had chosen me.

"Why did it choose you?" I asked.

"That, my dear, was a mystery to me."

"Oh." There were far too many mysteries around for my taste.

"Put that away and run along to bed. You've a big day tomorrow," she said, picking up her pen.

33

I ran into Francesca in the kitchens at noon the next day. She walked up to me, wearing her Princess's Girl's uniform and towing Kate in her wake.

"So you're still one of us?" she asked.

"Yes, I am," I told her, relishing the moment.

The Princess had reinstated me once she'd stopped kissing Prince Sterling. She'd written a royal decree naming me, Darling Wray Fortune, once again a Princess's Girl. She'd even stamped it with the royal seal. I had my things packed and ready to move back to the dormitory.

"So what's your job now, exactly?" Francesca demanded.

"I'm the new Under-assistant to the Wardrobe Mistress," I told her, beaming.

"Oh, you're just sewing," she said.

I shrugged; I'd spent my morning learning the fine art of embroidery. Not that I needed to, but Marci thought I might enjoy it. She was right. Turning silk thread into knots and flowers gave me a certain pleasure.

"And you?" I asked. "Are you back?"

"Yes," she said.

"Good," I replied.

She started in surprise. I wanted to say, *I never thought you did it,* but Kate interrupted.

"Ann's in hot water," she said. "Her mother got one look at those letters from her trunk and—"

"We don't squeal on other Girls, Kate," Francesca said. "Do we, Darling?"

"No, we don't."

She nodded to me and pulled Kate off to lunch. I spied Roger at a table and hurried over.

"What happened?" I hadn't seen him since we'd split up in the passage.

"Stuff," he said.

"Did you get caught?"

"Nope."

"Where'd you come out at?"

"The main Guard room," he said.

"And you didn't get caught?"

He grinned like an idiot.

"Talk," I said, poking him.

"Dulcie came flying in like her hair was on fire," he said. "They never noticed me."

"Huh," I said.

At that moment, Gillian came into the kitchens. Her dark curls bounced under their bright blue ribbon. She looked around, patting the embroidery on her Princess's Girl's apron pocket. She was still the Under-presser. She spotted us and waved.

I waved back.

She collected her lunch and sat with us.

"It's so exciting!" she said. "Well, all except for the part that there isn't a ghost!"

"Might be," Roger said.

"Really?" she breathed.

Roger stared at me. I stared back. He shrugged. Gillian deflated a little.

I reached into my pocket and dug out the key.

"Cherice dropped this," I told them, holding it out.

I'd shined it up so that it sparkled, all silvery and new-looking. Magnificent Wray's starburst shone on the key's bow. The tiniest hum of magic vibrated there. A mere morsel, but enough to whet my appetite for more. Whatever this key opened, it had to be important.

Gillian reached out, and I let it fall into her palm. She studied it.

"What does it open?" she said.

"I don't know."

"Too small for a door key," Roger said.

"Have you tried it in one?" she asked.

"Not yet. I thought you two could help me search," I said.

"What was Cherice doin' with it?" Roger asked.

"I think it's the reason she hid in the castle; she was looking for the lock it fits."

"But she had months to search. Wouldn't she have found it?" Gillian said.

"Maybe, but I don't think she did. She was ranting about her inheritance and the key when she was caught," I said.

"Hmm." Gillian turned the key over, examining it. "It might open something small, something hidden in something else . . . a jewel case, for instance."

"Jewels could be what she meant by inheritance," Roger said.

Cherice *had* ransacked the Princess's room and scattered her jewelry everywhere.

"Cherice said something about six and seven," I reminded Roger. "That might be a clue."

"Six and seven," Gillian muttered to herself, twisting a curl in thought.

"There's a million keyholes in the castle," Roger said. "It'll take time to try them all."

"We can take turns," I said.

"Can we?" Gillian's dimples deepened.

I nodded. She handed the key back to me. I stashed it in my pocket.

"Looks like there's plenty to search for this winter," Roger said. I knew he meant keyholes *and* secret doors.

"We'll get started tonight," Gillian said, reaching into her pocket. "But first, I got this for you."

She held out a slim gray volume.

"What's that?" I asked.

"It's a notebook, from the Baroness's library."

"How did you get this?" I asked, taking it.

The cover fell open. *My Father, Magnificent Wray,* the first page read, *by Lady Amber DeVere.*

"From Lady Kaye," Gillian said. "I knew you wanted to read the other book, and this isn't the same—"

"Thank you!" I exclaimed.

"You swipe that?" Roger asked.

"No, goose," Gillian said, tossing her curls. "I asked straight out. Darling, I said, wanted to know more about her family, and wasn't it sad that there weren't any books about it?"

"And she just gave it to you," Roger marveled.

"It's not like a jewel or anything," Gillian replied.

But it was. I hugged it close. It didn't have a whisper of magic in it, but it had answers. I couldn't wait to read it. Tears welled in my eyes. I'd never realized how good a friend Gillian was.

"About that ghost," I said. "We found the old woman's bones."

"What?" Gillian said, eyes ablaze.

"Have I got a story to tell you," I said. "But this one isn't made up. It's true. See, I found this closet. . . ."

And I told her the whole tale.

Acknowledgments

This is my favorite page of the entire book! Here I have the privilege of thanking you, my reader! If it weren't for you, I wouldn't write!

I want to honor the memory of my mother, Marjorie Maupin. Mom read to me, took me to the library each week, and insisted I be given my own library card. That card was gold to me!

Thank you to all the librarians in my life. You found me books, introduced me to the interlibrary loan program (important when you grow up in a small town), and shared your wealth of knowledge with me. I especially want to thank all of you who have championed and encouraged me as an author.

I have a marvelous group of people behind my books: my agent, Sara Crowe; my editor, Diane Landolf; Random House's Michelle Nagler and Mallory Loehr; book designer Liz Tardiff; publicists Cassie McGinty and Margret Wiggins; and the amazing sales and marketing teams. On top of all that, I have two fabulous illustrators, Lissy Marlin and Melissa Manwill.

Thanks to my family: Jon, Sara, and Rebecca. My good friend (and long-suffering listener) Faye Wade. My critique partners, Kaye Bair and Rachel Martin. My Ames posse: Sarvinder Naberhaus, Jane Metcalf, Kate Sharp, and Ann Green. Jill Friestad-Tate, the greatest encourager on the planet (if she can't make you smile, nobody can). Mary Guidicessi, Darling's own personal cheerleader.

And thanks be to God, who taught me not to be afraid of the dark.

TRY ON A LITTLE MORE MAGIC!

TURN THE PAGE FOR A SNEAK PEEK AT THE NEXT BOOK IN THE **100 DRESSES** SERIES!

1

Fog wrapped the castle. Not the cloudy vapor of an early-spring morning, but the fog of forgetfulness. It became as though thoughts of the past slipped through people's fingers. Oh, not that they couldn't remember when they tried, but more that they lost the desire to keep those memories.

I knew the dragons were to blame, because they were what people forgot the most. I'd mention them and receive a blank stare in response.

"Dragons?" they'd gasp, blinking in astonishment. "There is no such thing as dragons!"

How quickly they forgot. When my father, Magnificent Wray, had collared those dragons, they'd celebrated. When he'd set the dragons to build the Star Castle, they'd cheered. But when he passed away, the dragons became a myth in a matter of months. A foggy, uncertain idea that was best left unthought. Only a few

people retained the memories of those days. A handful held the
precious trickle of thoughts: vital notions of dragons, magic, and
danger.

I am one of the few.

—*Lady Amber DeVere,* My Father, Magnificent Wray

The key burned a hole in my apron pocket. It was small and silver, with a starburst inscribed on its bow. And although dozens of keys hung in the Head Steward's office, they were ordinary. None had a starburst. *This* key had once belonged to Magnificent Wray, my ancestor and the architect who had designed the castle. A man of mystery and magic. The starburst was his emblem, and that made this one special.

The bow held the smallest spark of magic. I hadn't noticed it until I pressed my thumb down hard, but it was there. Which made me wonder: Did the lock it fit hold a greater magic? A stronger, more powerful force? What would happen when the two met? And what lay behind that lock?

Did *this* key unlock a treasure?

That question fired my imagination with possibilities.

"Gold? Jewels? A magic ring?" I mumbled under my breath. "Magnificent Wray's secret workshop? *What?*"

"Quiet," Gillian whispered, peeking around the corner ahead of us.

I rolled my eyes. We were pressed against a wall outside the corridor to the Princess's suite. It was early, and everyone in the castle was busy getting ready for the day. Our chances of running into someone were small. But the past weeks of slinking around together looking for the keyhole had given Gillian a taste for stealth. She made each search an ordeal of hand signals, tiptoeing, hiding behind curtains, and flattening ourselves against walls.

It had gotten a bit ridiculous. But every keyhole beckoned, *Try me.*

Each chance we got, we hightailed it to the next tantalizing lock. One of us would be the lookout while the other tried the key. So far we hadn't had any luck. But Roger, the First Stable Boy, was right: it was too small to open doors. And we'd discovered it was too big to open jewel cases.

We were no closer to finding out what the key *did* open than we'd been when we started. There were at least a million locks in the Star Castle. We'd given the key to Roger, and he'd tried every keyhole in the stables and the outbuildings. Nothing. But it had to open *something*, and we planned to keep searching until we found out what.

Ahead of me, Gillian braced herself to sprint for the

next lock. Her dark curls were swept back with a ribbon, her brow furrowed in concentration. Her brown eyes fastened on the prize.

"On the count of three," she whispered. "One—"

"Three," I said, eager to arrive at the next lock.

I bounded around the corner and down the corridor. Past the ornate doors of the Princess's suite and straight to the double doors leading to the soon-to-be King's suite. It had been closed up since the death of Princess Mariposa's father, years earlier. Until now.

Gillian hurried to catch up with me.

"Darling, wait!" she called.

The doors to the King's suite were painted to resemble a view from a window. The painting portrayed Eliora by the White Sea, this very kingdom. The details were stunning. A mountain rose above the sea. Birds soared. Ships drifted in the harbor. The city sat nestled in its cove. And the Star Castle crested a rise that climbed to the mountain's top. I squinted at the brushstrokes: every leaf and stone was executed so that you felt you could reach out and touch it.

"It's a special kind of painting," Gillian said, panting a little. "Trumpet oil, Baroness Azure called it. I think that's a kind of paint. Anyway, it's supposed to fool you into thinking it's real."

Gillian had the habit of repeating what the Baroness told her. Although not necessarily correctly.

"Trompe l'oeil," I said. "It's a style, not a paint."

"Sure," she agreed affably.

She reached out and turned the castle, which rotated because it was actually the doorknob. The enameled metal piece fit so neatly into the painting that you didn't suspect it was there. She pulled the door open and walked inside.

"The Baroness said," she began, "that the Princess's suite used to be the Queen's suite when there was a queen. But now the Princess uses it, since she's like a queen. Only not. But she will be."

Princess Mariposa had stayed a princess since her parents' death because her father's will stated that she could be queen only upon her marriage. In a matter of weeks, there would be a wedding, a coronation, and a ball! The entire castle was abuzz over the upcoming events.

"I hope the Baroness said something we don't already know," I replied.

"She says lots of stuff." Gillian paused a moment to admire the suite's anteroom, with its three doors. "The King's suite is a mirror image of the Princess's."

A forest flowed around me, holding the walls, the floor, and the ceiling in its painted leafy embrace. The doors nearly melted into the walls. A bluethroat eyed me from its perch in a tree. The sun dappled its little brown head and the white-tufted blue patch under its beak. A rabbit hid in a hollow.

"The fastest way is to go straight through the bedroom," Gillian added.

She opened the center door, breaking the illusion, and stepped through. I followed her into a room devoid of furniture, where the scents of turpentine and lemon oil tickled my nose. The walls glistened with fresh paint: royal blue, Prince Sterling's favorite color. The carved crown moldings glinted with gold. The marble floor gleamed.

"It's being redecorated for Prince Sterling," Gillian explained, gesturing at the ladders and buckets scattered about the room. "New furniture, drapes, carpet. Well, all except for the reading room, of course."

"Uh-huh," I said.

"Prince Sterling declared that it was already perfect. He said don't change anything but the drapes," she continued, following me. "Mind your step."

I nearly stumbled over a rolled-up carpet. Gillian caught me with a grin. Threading our way around buckets and ladders, we reached the next door. Beyond it was a lounge. A partially finished mural wrapped the walls, but Gillian didn't waste time admiring it. She raced to the last door and threw it open.

"Here it is," she announced, as if I wouldn't grasp where I was. "The reading room!"

The King's reading room was a symphony of woods: maple, walnut, cherry, and mahogany. Polished parquet graced the floor. Carved panels braced the walls. Bare windows stared, wide-eyed without their draperies. A plush throne-sized chair sat next to a marble-topped table in the center, and a wonder of built-in bookcases and cabinets circled the room.

Silver keyholes winked at me from every door and drawer. *Untried* keyholes. The King's reading room: what better place to hide Magnificent Wray's treasure? My hand crept into my apron pocket and fastened around the key.

"Don't you want to curl up in that chair and read?" Gillian asked. "Well, I mean you would if the Prince's books were on the shelves. They will be soon—"

"Sure," I said, making a beeline to the nearest lock. "Watch the door."

I slid the key in and jiggled it. Nothing. I tried the next lock, and then another.

"Argh!" I exclaimed, shaking my fist at the cabinet. "One of you has *got* to open!"

Diving from lock to lock in a frenzy, I searched until I felt Gillian's hand on my elbow.

"My turn," she said with a smile that brought out her dimples.

I blinked, the key clutched in my fist. I was halfway around the room from where I had started.

"You look like a Laundress with a stubborn stain." She giggled.

I felt my face heat up. "Sorry," I said, handing her the key. "I got carried away."

"That's okay," she replied. "We do need to hurry. There are a lot more locks in here than I thought there'd be."

"Yes," I said a bit sheepishly.

"I'm starting to sympathize with Cherice," Gillian said.

Cherice, the former Wardrobe Mistress, had dropped the key when she was captured. She'd been hiding in the cellar, lurking in the castle's secret passages, so she'd had months—and before that maybe even *years*—to look. If finding the keyhole that fit the starburst key were easy, she'd have found it ages ago.

"It's got to be here," I said.

"If it is, we'll find it," Gillian replied.